The Spy Who Got His Feet Wet

By Marc Lovell

THE SPY WHO GOT HIS FEET WET
THE ONLY GOOD APPLE IN A BARREL OF SPIES
HOW GREEN WAS MY APPLE
APPLE TO THE CORE
APPLE SPY IN THE SKY
SPY ON THE RUN
THE SPY WITH HIS HEAD IN THE CLOUDS
THE SPY GAME
HAND OVER MIND
A VOICE FROM THE LIVING
THE SECOND VANETTI AFFAIR
THE BLIND HYPNOTIST
DREAMERS IN A HAUNTED HOUSE
AN ENQUIRY INTO THE EXISTENCE OF VAMPIRES
A PRESENCE IN THE HOUSE
THE IMITATION THIEVES
THE GHOST OF MEGAN

The Spy Who Got His Feet Wet

MARC LOVELL

PUBLISHED FOR THE CRIME CLUB BY
DOUBLEDAY & COMPANY, INC.
GARDEN CITY, NEW YORK
1985

All the characters in this book
are fictitious, and any resemblance
to actual persons, living or dead,
is purely coincidental.

LIBRARY OF CONGRESS CATALOGING IN PUBLICATION DATA
Lovell, Marc.
The spy who got his feet wet.
I. Title.
PR6062.O853S698   1985   823'.914   84-18713
ISBN 0-385-19940-6

The Spy Who Got His Feet Wet

CHAPTER 1

The hand appeared from nowhere. It plucked the envelope out of Apple's breast pocket. There was no finesse in the act; it had no suggestion of the pickpocket's smooth, covert skill. The hand appeared, grabbed, went.

For three seconds Apple stood still. His mind, caught dazedly between surprise and fear, was trying to find an explanation: thief? prankster? airport official? enemy?

Apple jerked into life on realising that the why of it didn't matter at the moment. Recovery was urgently desirable. He switched his head about like a lost child.

Appleton Porter was in one of Heathrow Airport's large concourses. Sheepishly following their own individual paths, people swirled around on all sides, some brushingly close. In among the mass of heads could be seen several eddies of haste.

The closest of these zoomed at Apple's attention. He noted that the maker was a man of about his own age (twenty-nine), with a bald crown among dark hair and a thin body in a creased blue suit; this while he was noting that a familiar envelope was being thrust into a pocket.

Appleton Porter moved into action.

As making a fuss was taboo—on a mission, you never called attention to yourself—Apple didn't bellow for someone to stop that thief. He simply gave subdued chase. His surprise had gone and his fear was being overtaken by excitement.

Like somebody with nothing on his mind except meeting a plane, Apple pushed through the crowd politely but firmly. He had no worry about losing the man ahead, for, despite the surrounding people, he had him in clear view at all times.

Appleton Porter was six feet seven inches tall.

And it was his height, Apple assured himself now, that was causing some people to glance his way, as happened to him every day and in every place; his act of being unflurried was perfect.

But Apple remembered, with pleasure at his daring, that today he wasn't wearing his usual drab suit. So clothing could be the attention-getter. It wasn't just any old time that you saw a man in a bright yellow blazer.

Grinning harshly, Apple went on across the concourse. He made no special effort to close the gap between the balding man and himself. This was because his logical half was telling him that recovery action ought to be taken only in a less crowded spot, perhaps over at the side there.

Apple didn't know what his emotional half was telling him: that he should extract whatever suspense and excitement he could out of this incident. There had been little enough of that in the past; there looked to be small hope of it in the present mission.

Although Appleton Porter had been an employee of British Intelligence since leaving university, rarely had he been used in the spy game, sent out into the frosty field as an agent on an operation. There were encumbrances.

First came his height. Apple was forced to agree with Angus Watkin, his control, as well as others in the world of Upstairs, that rendering himself unnoticeable in anything but a sit-down scene would be quite difficult, and an agent had to blend.

Second came his nature. It, unfortunately for his career,

tended to be sympathetic. No successful operative in the history of espionage had been less than low-level ruthless.

Third came his blushing. He was wont to colour up and become confused when touched on certain tender areas of his personality. The condition, he and Upstairs knew, was incurable, though an individual attack could sometimes be weakened by using psychological-physiological tricks. Spies did not blush.

Minor encumbrances, all carefully noted in the Appleton Porter dossier, were his low marks in lying, resistance to pain and dirty combat; plus, under REMARKS, the fact that he had a habit of collecting bits and pieces of useless information, which suggested a lack of security, just as those other minors suggested a feeble portion of self-confidence. Your three-star spook was secure and arrogant, a toughie.

Apple did look fairly tough at the moment. Jaw out, he had begun to forge through the crowd with more authority: not only was the balding man ahead getting close to the hall's side, but Apple had come to the conclusion that, prankster or official now obviously being out, the man had to be either a thief or an enemy.

Pulling for the latter, which could make for a lively caper, Apple started to close the intervening gap. He told himself that whatever the man's motive might be, the envelope had to be recovered, and a plane had to be caught. Take-off time was getting close.

The man in front glanced back. This was the first time he had done so. It put a brake on Apple's growing excitement, for he knew that if the man were in espionage, he, like Apple himself, would have been taught the best routine for a situation such as this:

If being followed in a crowd, never look behind. You could be gifting the tail with a positive identification—right when he was about to follow someone else.

Apple came up with the reminder, however, that the one who had grabbed his envelope could be putting on an act of gross amateurism in the hopes of covering his true status, which was even more promising.

The balding man reached the wall. There, passenger-use trolleys stood in an untidy line, many piled with the luggage belonging to the accompanying person.

Apple, free of the crowd, shot ahead at a near run. After another showing of his thin, grim face, the man twisted aside and leapt a trolley.

Apple started to do the same. At once, the man whipped back toward the trolley's tall handle and with a long reach gave it a shove.

The cart swung in a circle. Its handle hit Apple on the leg. Though mild in force, almost painless, the blow was enough to knock him off his mid-air balance.

Apple landed like a ballerina with housemaid's knee. He wobbled and fell. Lightly blushing a grade-one, he leapt up at speed. But, he was relieved to see, the mishap had not stretched the gap.

The way ahead was choked by two lines of trolleys. Most of them were loaded with baggage. The man in the creased suit was making poor progress in squeezing along between the piled and angled carts.

Apple followed. His face lost its pinkness.

Appleton Porter had a pleasant face and, to some, a good-looking one. It was as neat and standard as the collar and tie below, the short-cut gingery hair above. While his pale skin with its flick of freckles went along with the rest, his attractive green eyes hinted at a longing to escape from the neat and normal—as well as the condemning height and a limp personality.

Apple forged his way along the luggage-lined trench. As it had been widened slightly by the man in front, he made excellent time. He would, in fact, have continued appreciating the excitement and mechanics of the chase, except for the loudspeakers.

After a ping-pong bell, they began to murmur intimately. The sound was like someone talking through a rain of gentle kisses. Apple heard clearly only the word Dublin. It was enough.

Dublin was his destination. The delay, he thought, must be over. His plane was due to take off.

Apple discarded restraint like a burst glove.

Using his arms as oars on the piles of baggage, he began to hustle as fast as he could go. He didn't care whether or not he drew attention to himself; and when his rowing arms sent two suitcases to the floor, loudly, he winced only once.

The balding man's response to the noise was to shoot ahead over the last few feet of trench. He wrenched free of the trolleys. Darting, he went between people and then into a wide doorway.

When, seconds later, Apple passed through that doorway himself, he found he was in a corridor. Transients laden with suitcases moved in both directions.

The envelope thief was weaving quickly in and out of view among the trudgers.

Following, Apple went at a run. He assured himself that high haste was accepted, and even common, in places such as airports and stations. He accepted that it was also bad manners. But he did manage to mumble an excuse-me at some of those by whom he brusqued.

Suddenly, the gap between chaser and chased shrank. Apple

had come within touching distance of his man before he realised the reason: chased had reduced speed to a brisk walk. And
the reason for that, Apple saw, was three policemen.

The uniformed constables stood together, by the corridor
wall. They were sharing a read of a newspaper.

Snappingly, Apple both retracted his reaching hand and
slowed his run to a stride: on an operation, you avoided involve-
ments, especially with the police.

One behind the other, chased and chaser went on at a seemly
pace. They passed near the constables—who didn't glance up
from the racing results—and gradually increased their speed
until they were once again running and dodging.

The balding man led the way into another corridor. It had
merely a scattering of people.

Chased and chaser, throwing off the last masks of pretence,
leapt forward into an all-out gallop. They both growled with
determination.

Good runner though he was, it took Apple two more short
corridors to catch up, and at that it was because the thief lost
ground through looking behind him while rounding a corner.
Apple pounced.

There was a brief scuffle. Holding on with one hand, Apple
dipped into the pocket and located his envelope and yanked it
out.

Ripping himself free, the man ran off.

After putting the envelope away, safely, in an inside pocket of
his blazer, Apple paused, listening. From around the corner
behind him was coming a curious sound. It was a thudding and
a squeaking. He turned.

At that moment, two men burst into view at a run. They
collided with Apple. Everyone fell down.

While Apple, like the other two men, was picking himself silently and icily up from the floor, he noted the source of that curious thud-squeak sound: the strangers were wearing shoes that were soled with crêpe rubber.

Breathing unevenly, the three men stood formed in a small triangle. Somehow, Apple wasn't surprised when the heavier of the pair said, "We're Airport Security." He and his companion flipped over lapels to show identity cards.

Apple asked a cool "And?"

"We'd like to know why you and your friend were in such a hurry."

"What friend? I don't have any friends. I mean, I'm travelling alone."

"The hurry?"

"To catch the Dublin plane. It still is. The flight's just been called."

"That announcement was to advise of another thirty-minute delay for the Dublin departure."

"Oh."

"In any case," the same, heavy man said, "you were heading for Arrivals."

"Oh."

"Furthermore, you have no hand-baggage."

"I travel light," Apple said. "My cases're checked in, of course."

The men exchanged a look. Apple brought out his recovered envelope and showed its contents: airline ticket, boarding pass, stubs of baggage-checks.

With the urgency over, Apple was beginning to enjoy himself. He knew this standard scene. The heavy one would do all the talking while his partner glared with never a blink. The latter was supposed to be psychologically damaging to its recipient;

for its creator, as Apple also knew, it could mean either a headache or sore eyes.

The men were in their mid-twenties. Their suits, hair and faces looked to have been steam-pressed that morning.

The talker said, "Thank you, Mr. Teever." He had read the name on the ticket. "I'd like to see your passport, please."

Apple exchanged his envelope for the passport, which was nicely bent and wrinkled, even though it had been only one hour old when handed to him the day before.

Talker began to flip pages. Glarer went on glaring. Apple gave him an understanding smile.

"Your date and place of birth, sir?"

Apple recited the truth, because it matched, there having been no reason for changes there. Next, in answer to a question, he lied with "Yes, I'm an insurance salesman."

Apple was a professional linguist. He spoke six foreign tongues with absolute perfection, five more with fluency but an accent, and several others with competence.

"You live in Hove, Mr. Teever?"

"That's right."

False. He had a flat in Bloomsbury. He also owned a country cottage where he spent weekends with his Ibizan hound, Monico, who boarded weekdays with a local farmer.

Talker asked, "Your office is in Hove, sir?"

"Yes, it is."

False. He worked in Kensington, at the United Kingdom Philological Institute, where no one knew of the undercover part of his life.

Apple offered, "It's not exactly what you'd call an exciting job."

True. In neither part of his language work, straight nor spook, did he find stimulation, only a cerebral comfort. The work for Upstairs usually consisted of translations. Apple got more kicks out of his favourite reading, espionage fiction, which fed his determinedly romantic view of espionage reality.

Talker, it appeared, could think of nothing else to say, and Glarer's left eye was beginning to gather water.

Accepting and putting away his passport, Apple said, "Well, sorry to have taken up so much of your time."

Talker glared. Glarer said, "That's all right, sir. Good afternoon."

Five minutes later, Apple was back on the route he had been taking when the balding man had snatched his envelope. In connexion with that incident, Apple felt mildly disappointed. He suspected that the man was a common thief, of whom there were always plenty at airports.

Apple shrugged indifferently. No matter, he thought. He was here on the start of a caper, and he was wearing a blazer of screaming yellow.

Apple's love of the sartorially outrageous grew in relation to the distance he got from the time when he had been young enough to dare such anomalies; and never had so dared. It was for that reason that his car, Ethel, previously a London taxi, was painted lime green, orange and red.

Apple went on enjoying his bold appearance until he entered the departure lounge, where he halted on the threshold with his nerves tightening.

Not one of the many people present was wearing a bright yellow blazer.

Apple told himself in panic that it must be as he had suspected: the jacket was meant for official functions only, not as travelling wear. But he hadn't been able to resist.

While thinking this, Apple was feverishly preparing for the

blush which he knew had to start right now. He used the latest short-term cure that was being talked about in blushing circles.

You had to imagine you were dressed as a bear, inside a suit of thick fur, and that you were dancing on a box full of hot coals, at noon, in Cairo.

As with all the tricks which Apple had tried over the years, gimmicks whose efficacy had, like respect, faded with familiarity, this one was based on the theory that the attack of blushing would be overpowered by the imagined heat and stiflement.

Apple had used it before with success, though not on anything stronger than a grade-two. He wondered how strong this attack was going to be.

Apple had been in the bear-skin and madly dancing for several mini-seconds before that part of his mind realised he wasn't blushing.

Then parts jelled and he saw what he had already noted, and responded to coolingly: present but semi-hidden were two other men in yellow blazers. He was not the only one.

His nerves loosening, Apple walked on into the lounge. He felt even better when not one single person spared him a glance. A moment later he felt better still, when he had come to a waiting halt by a group of men. He felt, in fact, quite marvellous.

All the nearby men were close to seven feet tall.

When Apple was going down the steps of the United Kingdom Philological Institute, he saw a familiar face. It belonged to a man who sat at the wheel of a kerb-parked car.

Apple's heart thudded, as though he had just heard his number called in a lottery.

Albert yawned. He was an undersized, middle-aged Cockney with white hair, a chopping-block face and no reverence for anyone other than the man whom he served as bodyguard and chauffeur, butler and valet. As customary, he was wearing a blue boiler suit.

Apple forgot about the lunch he had been anticipating all morning. He strode to the car and bent over. Speaking clearly because of the closed window, he asked:

"Are you looking for me?"

Instead of leaning across to roll the window down, Albert, expression whimsical, cupped a hand to his ear. He moved his lips without making a sound.

Apple was in no mood for schoolboy humour. He had a lump of hope in his throat. Swallowing, he grabbed the door handle and pressed. The door was locked.

After another yawn, patently artificial, Albert stretched his arm out behind him. He unlocked the rear door, which Apple then pulled open with "Do I get in?"

Albert inclined his head. "Dead right. Though I reckon as two into one won't go."

"I get in," Apple said, doing that. He closed the door but stayed on the seat's edge. "What's up?"

"Don't ask me, mate. I only work here."

"Albert, you talk too much."

Nodding, the older man started the motor. "Hold on slack," he said. "This is going to be a gentle ride."

Apple leaned back as the medium-size plain grey car moved off slowly. It joined the traffic, which looked more sluggish than it was, due to being gilded with spring sunshine.

His hope happily digested, its realisation obviously in the offing, Apple began to hum. At the same time, to keep his mind from building a fabulous, high-level caper, he started going through foreign languages to find their equivalents of REMARKS.

Some minutes later Apple was still humming and seeking,

though he was now after equivalents of MOST SECRET, when the car drawled to a halt.

It was in a space at the kerb that was reserved for buses. Apple wondered if Upstairs had something on London Transport. He was only part joking.

But the stay was brief. They were moving again as soon as the new passenger had closed himself in. He settled with a lazy "Let there be peace, Albert."

Formally, the driver said, "Yes, sir."

From the back of the front seat arose a glass partition. Apple watched the growing reflection of Angus Watkin, his control from Upstairs.

Like the car, Watkin was medium-size and ordinary to look at, and for the same reasons. Aged between forty-odd and fifty-plus, he had a blendable face and nondescript hair. His suit and shoes, shirt and tie were drably neat.

Angus Watkin was the type of man who could loiter in a conspicuous doorway for an hour, and no one among those observant few who actually noticed him would wonder about it.

When the glass had slotted into place, Apple said, being tradecraft correct, "Good morning, sir." You said good morning until twelve, good day until one, and good afternoon thereafter. It was taught in Signals Three.

"Porter," Angus Watkin said with a glance aside, thus acknowledging his underling's presence, "there are no telephones in operation at your place of employ."

"The whole street's out for the day, sir."

"Therefore I had to use that untidy method of making a contact. I do hope you weren't inconvenienced, that I haven't dragged you away from something important."

Cheerfully ignoring the sarcasm, Apple said, "I'm always delighted to renew old acquaintances." He had seen no one with an Intelligence connexion for months.

"Good," Angus Watkin said. Without a pause he added, "I have a little errand for you."

In spookspeak, both that noun and its adjective had reversed values, as was also the case with big operation, which term meant that you stood in cold darkness for hours in order to take the licence number of a car that might not go by tonight.

Clenching his toes in deep satisfaction, Apple told his chief's ghost in the glass, "Thank you, sir, for giving me this opportunity."

"You have the two qualities that are vital to this mission, Porter."

"I have?"

"Yes. Tallness and Russian."

"Oh," Apple said flatly, but his spirits refused to be brought down. A caper was a caper, no matter what the reason for his being used on it. He asked:

"Is it a team job, sir?"

Angus Watkin shook his head. "It's all yours, Porter. Your number-name for this mission is One."

Apple turned to the window in case his stimulation showed. His physical dither he hid by shuffling. In charge of himself again, he turned back with a crisp:

"Very good, sir."

Watkin said, "You are One from now until you return from abroad."

"Abroad where?" Apple asked, quickly, before his mind had time to start picturing the distant and exotic. He was thus only marginally let down to be told that his destination was Dublin, a thirty-minute flight away.

"Know what's happening there next week, Porter?"

Apple tapped his brow, anxious to shine. Semi-guessing, he said, "Some kind of sports deal."

"Basketball," Angus Watkin said, his voice silky because he was on the knowing end. "It's an international competition, a friendly as opposed to an official, with a dozen or so countries participating, including the United Kingdom."

"Yes, sir, I remember now."

"How much of an expert on the game are you, Porter?"

That was typical. Another person would have phrased it: "Know anything about the game?" This Watkin phrasing was a Watkin cruelism. He often pretended to expect a 10 so that even an excellent 8 could be derided. Apple realised he ought to have displayed disappointment over the mission's locale.

But he showed his independence by not bothering to pretend, saying, "I know absolutely nothing about basketball."

Angus Watkin recovered beautifully. He said, "Good."

Apple gave a mental sigh. He told himself he had his nerve, trying to get the better of the odious Watkin in these subtle battles. He asked why it was good. The way he pronounced sir was like a hiss.

"Learning the hows and whys of the game should keep you safely occupied over the next three days. You are not, one trusts, averse to a stay in the country."

"Not at all, sir, no."

Angus Watkin folded his arms, slowly, like a teacher determined to get to the bottom of it all. Showing his dull profile, he looked out at the passing townscape.

"As you may possibly have divined by now," he said, "you are going to be sent to Dublin with the British contingent."

His mouth sagging, which rendered the words sloppily formed, Apple asked in an incredulous voice, "I'm going to play basketball for Britain?"

"Don't be ridiculous, Porter."

Apple settled. "Sorry, sir."

Angus Watkin said, "At Damian House they'll tell you the rules and lore and strategies, not teach you to be a world-class player."

"Certainly not."

"You will go as a reserve, of whom there are several. One fervently hopes that, for the honour of one's country, you will not be called upon to play."

"Quite so, sir."

Angus Watkin patted himself gently on the biceps. This gesture seemed to say, There now, try not to lose patience with the dolt.

Apple said, "I imagine, sir, that this mission concerns the Russian contingent."

"The mission," Angus Watkin said like a deaf man, "concerns the Russian contingent."

"Really?"

"Among the players and reserves, coaches and trainers, public relations people and assorted hangers-on, there is a person who would like to establish contact with British Intelligence."

"I see, sir."

"The idea being to sell information. At least, that is the way the rumour comes through."

"I see, sir," Apple said again. It had an efficient ring to it, he thought.

Watkin said, "I won't bore you with details." That, as Apple knew, was Watkinese for *I wouldn't tell you this under duress.* "Suffice it to say that the field has been narrowed to three people."

"Which makes my job a trifle easier."

"I shall give you their names anon. The three are the only ones who could possibly have access to information."

"Through their high-placed jobs, I suppose, sir, or membership in the Communist Party."

Angus Watkin looked around. "No, Porter. Most of these sports people are too young to be in positions of consequence. The players themselves are, of course, in their late teens or early twenties."

"Naturally," Apple said with a firm nod, as if he had only been kidding.

"It is the trio's fathers who are in high positions, and the assumption is that the information will be passed on innocently from parent to rebellious child."

"That sounds a likely situation, sir."

"It does," Angus Watkin said. "But that is all I can tell you about the matter."

"Yes, sir. Need-to-know."

"No, Porter: need of knowledge. I possess no more than I have given you, save for one not-encouraging item. It's another rumour."

"How strong, sir?"

"Strength five against the original's strength eight. And it has it that the would-be traitor has changed his mind."

"Let's hope not, sir," Apple said—brightly, to counter his slight feeling of queasiness at the word *traitor*.

"You'll soon find out when you've made contact with the trio and isolated the right one," Angus Watkin said as though that task were as simple as lighting three cigarettes from a single match.

"Yes, sir. But if the first one I approach tumbles that I'm an operative, he's fairly sure to pass it on to the team's KGB watchdogs."

"It's likely, yes."

"So how do I make contact? How do I keep him in the dark until I feel it's safe to switch the light on?"

Angus Watkin turned away again to face the passing scene. "That, Porter," he said, "is your problem."

The remainder of the journey to Ireland would have been placid except for the inner Apple. He sat between a snorer and a reader, neither one a member of the British basketball team entourage, the tallest of whom stood in the aisle for most of the flight.

Too shy to join these stars, Apple suffered spasms of claustrophobia as well as the discomfort of having his knees jammed hard against the seat in front.

Another factor that kept him sitting was his desire to be only a background figure in the sports group. He didn't want to have to answer too many questions.

Apple had met everyone concerned yesterday, at a reception in London. The other players had been polite. They appeared to accept without protest that John Teever, an unknown, had been selected as a reserve by the powers that be in the world of British basketball.

But Apple knew that his cover was frail in respect of the game. So he needed to keep himself to himself except for those official occasions when he had to be with the others. He had to stay an outsider.

Which is how Apple began to feel toward the end of the flight, with his colleagues exchanging the jokes and insults of their companionship.

Apple's mild gloom reminded him that the mission he had undertaken was not exactly of the first water. It lacked style, intrigue and danger, and would be no earth-shaker even if brought to a successful conclusion.

Apple told himself, however, that any caper was infinitely better than no caper; that he was, after all, a One; and that your strength-eight rumour was next door to the nearly true, which was sometimes believable.

Apple grew cheerful again on the team's chartered bus into town. Holding not only the British entourage but also a score of reporters, Irish and foreign, it was a jocular riot on wheels. A respectable percentage of the pressmen were sober.

Most of the talk and crush took place near the front of the bus, where the stars were gathered. Aisle action eased off rearward through trainer, manager, medic, masseur and the assorted nobodies. Apple sat on the back seat with a bland ballcounter.

So as not to think of being an outsider again, Apple reminded himself aptly that the expression "beyond the pale" was born here in Dublin. Before Cromwell's time, the Pale had been the area under English domination; anyone beyond the boundary was considered an enemy or a peasant.

That mental fondling over with, his infomania pampered, Apple went on to muse that here he was, an outsider again.

He was diverted by a reporter. The man, tail-ender of the press gang, moved back with a yawn to strap-hang above Apple, who thought: American.

Signs were a suit light in colour and loose in fit, glints of bridgework, British-style shirt that the British male no longer wore, and the tawny, dried-out skin that was a side effect of central heating.

Accent matched when he said, "How're you today?" A youthful forty, he had short fair hair and a hawk face. He was tall.

"Fine thank you fine," Apple said at a brusque trot, hoping to end it there. He needed press attention like he needed more freckles.

"You must be on the team," the man said.

"Oh?"

"That jacket."

Apple kept his head down. "Reserve."

"Really?"

The word was so potently pronounced that Apple looked up. He said, "Yes, really."

"Maybe you'd care to comment on this whisper I heard at the airport, Mr. . . . ?"

"Draper," Apple double-lied.

"Right. They call me Scoopsy. It's supposed to be cute. But this whisper."

"I don't know anything."

"It says that there's animosity by the team against a substitute reserve, because he replaced an old friend of theirs. Is that true?"

"I don't know a thing."

The reporter bragged about his dentist's bill. "Say, maybe *you're* the substitute, Mr. Reaper."

"Neeper," Apple corrected amiss. "No, I'm not. And the original man is sick, hence the replacement."

"Way I heard it, he's totally fit and this was to be his last big international game before he retired from competitive basketball."

"Sick. Like me."

The reporter asked a startled, "What?"

Putting a hand limply to his forehead, Apple said, "I'm going to be sick."

The man called Scoopsy backed off. "Bye, Mr. Beacon."

"Goodbye," Apple said in relief, not caring that his seat companion, the ball-counter, was edging away.

Relief lasted until guilt became too strong to continue unrecognised, a period of roughly two minutes. Wincing, Apple faced up to the fact that he had taken a healthy man's valued place. Dublin was to have been his final bow, his last glimpse of the limelight, his swan song. He had been cheated. He was a victim.

Apple allowed his guilt to go on. He preferred it to the facing of another fact, one which he skittered around with frequency: in the machinations of the spy game, innocent non-players generally suffered more than the players themselves, while leaving out the Upstairs' strategists completely, for their only suffering might, or might not, be remorse.

It wasn't Apple's guilt about this additional fact that made him hold it off; it was fear of damaging the romantic view he held of the espionage world.

Squirming at visions of a tall man in despair about what would never be, Apple reached for his cigarettes. In time, he remembered that basketball players were supposed to be free of the tobacco habit, so he could indulge only on the quiet. He squirmed.

Presently, relief came again on Apple's finding escape. He had recalled the first part of Scoopsy's whisper: the team's animosity. Apple considered that in connexion with what had happened at the London airport.

It would, he thought, be possible to pay a thief to grab the unknown reserve's ticket. But far easier to get a friend to do the job. There would be no danger. If caught, the culprit could laugh it off as a joke, with the team's collaboration, thus satisfying both police and substitute reserve.

That's what it could have been all about, acknowledged Apple with a sigh for the dullness of the possibility, the stars trying to avenge a player-friend while hoping to make the usurper miss his plane.

Feeling abused, which made a change from the guilt, Apple looked out of the window at Dublin's fair city.

It was raining.

Apple felt sorry for people who were neurotic; therefore he accepted it without rancour when, at the hotel, he was ignored by the others; also when either design or happenstance arranged it so that he was last to be attended to at the reception desk. Instead, he reflected on how well he was doing at keeping in the background.

Apple went up three flights of stairs in the old, rambly building. On the passage he turned along, all the doors were closed. Key in one hand, suitcase in the other, he halted at number thirty-five.

In the middle of a stoop from having put his case down, Apple froze. His head near the door, he could hear beyond it a fumbling sound. He moved closer.

Over the following seconds, excited, Apple listened to various stealthy sounds while quietly gentling his key into its lock. Then, in one swift movement, he unlocked and pushed open the door, stood erect and stepped inside.

The maid screamed.

A yard from the door, she was obviously about to leave the room, her arms full of cleaning canisters and cloths. Face aghast, she clutched her burden.

Glaring a smile of reassurance, Apple put out his hands in motions of calm and told the stricken woman loudly that everything was all right.

Five minutes later, maid gone and incident brutally dismissed, Apple had put away his clothes and was looking around the room, which was cat-swing small but owned a seven-foot bed.

On the vanity table lay a list of hours: meals, games, social events and the rehearsal tomorrow morning of the afternoon's opening ceremony. Apple committed the list to memory. That this was totally unnecessary he declined to admit; the act gave a warm, spy-like feeling.

After a wash in the attached bathroom, Apple lit a cigarette. The smoke, he enjoyed more than usual because of its illicit, stolen-fruit quality.

Cheerful and alert, Apple left his room and went down to the lobby. There he was buttonholed by one of the team officials. The man tried to steer him into the dining hall, where the rest were eating, but accepted the story that he had snacked on sandwiches upstairs.

Apple went outside, into a square which had a surrounding of elegant buildings. Street-lamps gleamed in the gloaming like twinkly eyes. The rain had stopped.

Strolling toward O'Connell Street, three blocks away, Apple wondered for the first time about a One-watcher. Even though he hadn't been given a back-up man for this caper, there was almost sure to be an observer on hand. Angus Watkin liked to know what was going on.

Rain began to spatter. Apple changed to a jog. He kept it up until, after crossing O'Connell Street (one of the widest main thoroughfares in the world, he recalled, along with Canal in New Orleans), he drew near to the hotel that housed the Soviet visitors.

Across the street from it, in shelter from the rain under a tree, stood two policemen and another man. The latter, shabby and bearded, held a placard which asked that Afghanistan be borne in mind. Watching from several feet away, the policemen looked worried that he might go on doing nothing else but that.

Apple went into the hotel.

The large lobby was crowded, with a sprinkling of tall men among the mass of obvious tourists, including Orientals. Apple stayed in an inconspicuous spot near the door, where there was a constant coming and going.

He was hoping to pick out one of his three prospects, the only one whom he could recognise, having seen several press photographs in recent days. Yek Milyukov, twenty years old, was six feet six inches tall, had dark hair and a droopy moustache.

An hour passed. Nothing happened except for two teenage tourists asking Apple if he was somebody famous. He went out to find a snack bar.

That was simple. There were three fast-fooders just along the street, each belonging to a rival American chain. To spite himself, Apple chose the most garish. He was disappointed to discover that his giant hamburger was delicious.

Back in the hotel, he saw his number-one prospect straight away. Yek Milyukov stood talking to a girl in the middle of the room. Following a minute of fixing the real-life Yek in his mind, Apple gave all his attention to the girl.

She was tall. Rarely had Apple seen a woman of such a height —and he changed positions twice in order to get a clear sighting through the crowd and verify that she wasn't standing on something. He reckoned that she could be no more than four inches shorter than the man she was with.

The girl had short brown hair (flat hairstyle and flat footwear, thought Apple, who knew all the tricks of subtle height-reducing). Her round face had pretty features. She wore a uniform dress in red, which showed that she was part of the Soviet entourage.

Aware that 74 percent of doctors in the U.S.S.R. were female, Apple reckoned that the girl was probably a nutritionist or a medic or a physical therapist.

He wished his lip-reading were better so that he could know what she and Yek Milyukov were talking about. Matters of no consequence, he supposed, however, since neither looked to be particularly animated.

The girl left Yek with a brisk, Russian handshake and went from sight in the crowd. After a sigh, Apple told himself: back to business.

All he did, however, was go on watching Yek Milyukov, who was soon in conversation with someone else—by his jacket, a member of the Swedish team.

The reason Apple didn't try to make an approach to the Soviet player was twofold. One, he hadn't yet thought up a story to go with that approach; two, he wanted to draw the caper out as long as possible.

Even so, Apple started to get urges to act. He thought he ought to go over there and blunder it out, say whatever came into his head. Even if he didn't get very far, he would have established the beginnings of a relationship. He could go to work from that.

Apple was still undecided when he heard a voice beside him say, "Well, hello again, Mr. . . . um . . ."

It was the reporter, Scoopsy, with his bridgework. Apple, thinking it better not to give a double-lie this time, said, "John Teever."

"Right. I never forget a name."

Apple heard himself ask, "You don't happen to know the one that belongs to that tall girl who's with the Russian group, do you?"

"Tall girl with the Reds?" Scoopsy said. His hawk face perked with interest. "What girl? Hey, is there a romance going on all around me?"

Apple huffed, "No no, nothing like that."

Listening only to himself, the American reporter went on, "Now, that would be a story, if you like. Romeo and Juliet in modern dress. Boy on British team and girl on the Russian. Madly in love, but they can only wave to each other across a hotel lobby. And so forth."

"No no no," Apple said, sliding off. He was furious with himself for that stupid question. All he needed was to get into the newspapers.

"What did you say her name was?"

"I was asking for a friend."

Scoopsy said, "If she's pretty instead of one of those hulks, it's drinks all around."

"You're mistaken about this," Apple said. "Good night." He turned and strode twistingly between people to the entrance. Out in the rain, he started to run.

By the time he reached his own hotel, Apple had stopped having visions of his photograph spread across a newspaper's front page. Paranoia had retreated in the face of derision.

Getting his key from the desk, Apple crossed the lobby, which was as bustling as the one he had left. He noted that some of the team seemed to be having an uproarious time in the bar. He trotted upstairs with his chin high.

Outside room thirty-five, Apple paused. He listened through the wood. It was quiet inside. He opened the door—and then he paused again.

On seeing the mess, Apple felt both shock and hidden pleasure.

From bedding to clothes, everything had been thrown about, though nothing seemed to be torn or damaged. A sheet lay in the bathroom doorway, a shirt hung from the ceiling light, his suitcase was on a picture-hook, sneakers sprawled on the naked mattress. There was a care about distribution which suggested prank rather than attack.

Apple declined to think into the significance of that. As he set about righting his room, humming, he recalled an item from Training Four.

If you wanted to search an enemy's quarters and wanted to hide that act—supposing that you weren't an expert—the best way was to do the reverse of the professional: instead of leaving everything precisely as was, make as much mess as you could. The suggestion would be a practical joke, a common thief, or foraging children.

Therefore, Apple thought, if the KGB had sent people here to nose about, they would have found nothing whatever to interest them. John Teever was as unimportant as was implied by his peripheral standing.

This Apple thought only vaguely, however. Another section of his mind was grappling for a word that had passed through a moment or two before.

Finally, the word came.

Reverse.

Apple nodded and sat on the bed. He mused that of the two reasons he had been employed on this mission, Russian language and height, the former had the most importance, with every nuance of speech counting, whereas his tallness was mere stage-dressing. So what he could do was reverse Angus Watkin's point, initially, and use Russian that was not perfect but quite awful.

Apple nodded again, as well as briefly folding his arms to give himself a hug.

He would approach Yek Milyukov, he thought, with the story

that he was a language student who wanted to practice his beginner's Russian. Few things flattered a Soviet more than a foreigner going to the trouble of trying to learn his native tongue —or anyway, the major tongue of a region where one hundred and forty-odd languages were spoken. Further flattery could be given by the student's rapid progress.

Things were getting brighter all round, Apple thought. He rose and stepped over a pillow to the window. After looking at the reflection of an abused room, he turned his attention to the outdoors below.

Apple smiled. He told himself that here he was, in a foreign capital, in a hotel room, gazing down onto a lamp-lit, rain-swept street.

CHAPTER 2

Harp Hall, in a suburb, was a new indoor stadium with seating for twelve thousand. It served for all the small ball-games, from tennis to billiards.

This morning, transposing the normal, the seats were mostly empty and the playing court was packed. Below, in addition to the competing teams and their entourage fragments, there were press people, staff, sneakers-in, local bandsmen minus glitter and instruments, and a hassle of the competition's organizers.

More of the last were up in the seating, having a private argument, which, it appeared, was being whipped along by the roar of the crowd below.

Variations on this theme by Bedlam had been going on for an hour. Apple was growing leg-weary from standing around among his noncommunicative colleagues—between bouts of marching and wheeling and bumping into other people.

Apple accepted as highly improbable that all this could result in a smooth opening ceremony, one which then had to be cleared away so that the first game of the play-offs could get started.

The tall Russian girl, Apple had not seen. Normally he would have had no trouble in pinpointing somebody in a crowd, but this crowd was made up predominantly of the super-tall. Apple had not been bored over the past hour.

Yek Milyukov he had glimpsed frequently. The Soviet athlete

appeared to be in excellent spirits, laughing and joking with others of his squad. Apple liked that from a professional viewpoint. The Service adage went: if you want the man with something on his mind, look for the one who laughs.

After an electronic squeal that made Apple's teeth dither, loudspeakers began to boom. Source was an official up in the seating area.

Not listening beyond the opening sentence, Apple was reminded of his shrewdness this morning at the hotel. He had realised that the disarranged room could be a distraction as well as a cover; that, in fact, his secret visitor could have been there to plant microphones. Apple had enjoyed the following search, even though no bugs were uncovered.

The official at the microphone talked on. The crowd below kept reasonably quiet except for the interpreters in each group of non-English-speakers. Apple got the message by listening to a nearby Norwegian, whose language was easier for him to understand than the official's Cork-flavoured English.

After that, the crowd went back to marching. Another hour passed before everyone was satisfied and the rehearsal ended. People began to disperse, the various nationalities started to fraternise freely, and Apple set off to edge his way toward the Soviet contingent.

The going was slow but sure. Apple weaved smilingly between the visitors, heading for his goal.

When almost there, and with Yek Milyukov in his sights, Apple saw a Hammer and a Sickle. Far shorter than the present average, the male and female KGB watchdogs had been hidden until now, up close. Lapel badges identified them as official interpreters.

For Apple, what identified the pair as KGB field personnel, apart from bland features and artificial smiles, was their skill at dividing their attention. Although talking to team colleagues, they kept their eyes busily on the move elsewhere. Also, each appeared to be tuning in to the other's conversation.

Apple veered off-course, away from the Soviet watchdogs. He wanted to delay as long as possible the bringing of himself to their notice. To hope for no attention at all from these professionals would be unrealistic.

Yek Milyukov and others were being photographed by media people. Most newspaper interest here was directed toward either the U.S.S.R. team or that from the U.S.A., joint favourites to reach the final.

Circling the photographers, who were beginning to lens other players, Apple got back onto course. He closed in on the man with the droopy moustache and fell into step at his side.

Milyukov looked around with a polite smile. The smile grew rapidly warmer as its owner read "fellow player" in the newcomer's appearance.

Putting on what he hoped was a shy expression, Apple said the equivalent in Russian of:

"Excuse me, please. My name is John. I am being a student of the beautiful Russian language. Will you like—I mean mind—if I talk to you for one minute about? I am desirous of obtaining practice." As well as his construction being awkward, his accent was terrible. Neither was easy to accomplish, for it went against the grain for him to misuse a tongue in which he was proficient.

Yek had stopped. His smile now happy, he put out a hand and said in his own language, "That's wonderful, John. I'll be very pleased to talk to you."

After the ritual of a formal hand-shake, Apple, the KGB watchdogs in mind, drew his prospect forward again.

He said, "Thank you, Yek. If I was able to call you by your first name. You are most generous. May I tell you about myself?"

"Please do."

Apple talked on, filling in his cover background and profession. He rounded off, "And my male parent is one who designs aircraft for the government."

"Mine," Yek said, "is a chemist of the industrial variety. As for myself, I'm still slaving away at university. I'm studying law."

"Slaving?" Apple asked, pretending not to understand. For one thing, he couldn't resist the political dig; for another, he wanted to get Yek Milyukov to talk more, for listening is flattery.

The basketball player talked. Meanwhile, Apple gently steered him further away from his national group, many of whom, Apple noted with satisfaction, were similarly in conversation with non-Russians. The Hammer and Sickle were safely busy, their eyes on the hop.

Apple and Yek went through an arch below the seating. They came out into the broad reception area, which circled the entire inner core of the building. There were scores of other people in the vicinity.

The one minute had already become about seven, Apple cheerfully reckoned. Which meant that he was doing far better than he had expected.

But time was limited, Apple knew, so he ought to start on the build-up to the point of this budding relationship, namely Yek Milyukov's possible sale to British Intelligence of information that he had wheedled out of his unsuspecting father. That, of course, would come later. It would be enough here to get things moving in the right direction.

Into a pause in the Soviet athlete's talk, Apple dropped a laconic, "You know, my father never tells me anything about his work."

Yek blinked. "Is that right?" He had been talking of using certain verbs in a figurative sense.

"It is," Apple said. He also blinked, pretending to be affected by sentiment. "I think people is very lucky who have parents who tell them things."

"I understand," Yek said with a sympathetic smile. He patted Apple on the shoulder.

Your average Russian, as Apple was well aware, had a disposition that was uncommon among the world's races. On first meeting he either liked you at once, and for always, or he found you less appealing than a fly in cold gravy.

Since by his mien it was patent that Yek Milyukov had taken to the language student, Apple became more cheerful, in respect both of himself and of the mission. At the same time, however, he felt blameworthy because of his act. He was performing a lie for someone who liked him.

A youth came up. He bore an autograph book as if it were a licence to waylay. Apple's annoyance slackened off when, finished with Yek, the youth turned to him with "Could I have yours, too, please?"

For the first time in his life, Apple signed an autograph book, albeit with a phony name. It didn't do a lot for him.

The youth left.

Walking Yek on, Apple began to talk. He wasn't aware that his accent and grammar had improved.

What Apple monologued about was family relationships, both good and mouldy. The words he used most often, however, had little to do with the subject. They were *information* and *sell*.

Apple told himself that he was doing beautifully. The build-up was coming along a treat. Also it was good that he had stopped having that absurd feeling of blame. Perhaps at last he was beginning to get harder.

Yek had started to shoot him quick glances, Apple saw. He wasn't sure if they were born of curiosity or puzzlement; but they did show that the Russian knew about the conversation's change to two levels.

Apple dropped his voice to a more intimate tone. He became absorbed in discovering how many different ways he could introduce his two words of import.

Again Yek came to a stop, causing Apple to do likewise. They stood close. This Apple liked for the way it created the required, secretive ambience.

So it came as a blow when now Yek Milyukov started edging backwards. Expression uneasy, he mumbled that he had to be going, he had enjoyed the chat, he hoped that the study of Russian would go on, he . . .

Turned away quickly and strode off.

Apple, slumping, let him go. He realised what this must mean. Yek had got the drift right enough, but he was not the rumour's protagonist. Wisely, he had left before getting too involved in what could be dangerous.

Through the glass outer wall, the British contingent could be seen boarding the bus. Apple headed that way. He reminded himself that he hadn't failed; he had eliminated one of the trio; that was progress.

He would seek one of the remaining pair later, Apple thought. To try it now would be giving his image far too much exposure in respect of the Hammer and Sickle. But would Yek tell the KGB attachment of his odd conversation with the British player?

Since lunch would only be a repeat of breakfast, insofar as cordial relationships were concerned, Apple mused on alighting from the bus at the hotel, and since he wanted to maintain a distance from the others anyway, he would go straight up to his room. Then, after a smoke on the sly there, he would go out and eat somewhere. Next, he would walk to the stadium for the opening ceremony, be on hand for when the Soviets arrived.

Apple went upstairs. It wasn't until he was covering the final yards to his room, humming, that he noticed its door. It stood wide open.

Not again, Apple thought, leaving off the hum. This could get to be a habit.

The last yard he covered with care, his upper body leaning forward so that he could get an early look inside. He dismissed the notion that possibly he looked peculiar.

On seeing a man in the room, Apple straightened and stopped.

The man rose casually from his seat on the bed. He was big. Not overly tall, but big. With a flat nose and a scarred jaw, wearing a threadbare raincoat, he could have passed for a bouncer who, due to middle-age, was beginning to find himself out on the pavement.

Impassively, Apple said, "I do hope I'm not interrupting anything here."

With a friendly shake of his head and a mild smile, the man said, "Not at all, Mr. Teever."

"I should hate it if I were to inconvenience anyone, Mr. . . . ?"

"Malone," the big man said. "Jack."

"Charmed, I'm sure."

"I'm with Security."

"Hotel?"

"State," Jack Malone said. He produced and held forward an identity card.

Apple said brackishly, "I don't know if I'm supposed to feel honoured or worried." He felt the latter. "Do I pose a threat to the nation?"

"Not so far as I know, Mr. Teever," Malone said. "And in any case, despite that very English name, you've got a look of the Irish about you."

"Only in my top lip, I believe," Apple said. "It was willed to me by an Irish grandmother."

"Is she still alive?"

"I'm afraid not."

"God rest her soul."

"Thank you."

"And congratulations," the big man said. "With a touch of the Irish in you, you can't go wrong." Before putting the identity card away, he placed it edgewise across his lips and blew a short whistle.

That took Apple's fancy, which annoyed him. In a peevish tone he asked, "Would it be all right with you, Mr. Malone, if I came in?"

"Of course. Feel free."

Apple went over the threshold. "I've got a suspicion," he said, "that if I wait long enough I'll learn the purpose of this unlawful visit."

"Unlawful, Mr. Teever?" the big man said pleasantly. "Well now, I'm sure you know that old expression about all being fair in love and war."

Apple replied that he was involved in neither. He told himself that he was playing the scene right: respectable bloke being walked over by brute authority.

As though Jack Malone had read his mind, he said, "Yes, well done."

At which point Apple recalled an old Service signal, now in retirement. To inform of a second significance in a matter/person/situation/object, you created a double effect, using any manner that was non-verbal. Among many possible ways was splitting a whistle.

Even so, Apple was surprised when the big man said, "Mr. Watkin asked me to call." He quoted Apple's Service number before adding, "He thought it might be a good idea if you got a look at me."

Recovering like a pro, Apple gave a cool nod. "How do you do, Mr. Malone."

"Hello again, Mr. Teever. Though I don't suppose that's your real name."

Aghast at the crassness of this in espionage terms, while concurrently sympathising with Malone for it, Apple nevertheless took note of the reminder that here could be one of Angus Watkin's sneaky little trials—testing anything from good manners to loyalty, and spycraft to sobriety.

It was also possible, Apple thought, that Malone was no more an officer of state security than John Teever was a first-class basketball player.

The big man gave up waiting for a response to his crude question-as-statement. He said genially, "It's grand wet weather, eh?"

Apple said, "Perhaps you have a message for me."

"No. Nothing like that."

"And you're not my back-up man?"

"No. I'm only your local contact with HQ—should such contact be called for."

"I hope it won't."

Jack Malone delved into a pocket and brought out a slip of paper. "This is the pertinent telephone number," he said. Not reading the digits aloud for them to be memorised, as expected, he passed the paper across, one outstretched hand to another.

Apple drawled a Watkin-like "Thank you, Mr. Malone."

"It was my pleasure, Mr. Teever," the big man said. "And that concludes my business." He came forward, passed Apple and moved into the doorframe, where he stopped.

He said, "I'm sorry that when you arrived you found me sitting down on the job."

Apple turned. "That's all right."

"The thing is, I was resting from tidying up the room. You're the messiest man I ever met." He gave a one-finger salute. "So long."

Apple closed the door. First he memorised the telephone number; next he burned the slip of paper over the lavatory bowl and flushed away the charred remains; last, and best of an enjoyable three, he lit a cigarette.

All Apple thought of in connexion with the room's repeat assault was to hope that word of it wouldn't reach Angus Watkin via his local people. Watkin could well interpret it as the underling having been rumbled by the opposition, and pull said underling out.

Smoking his cigarette with leisurely greed, Apple reflected how understandable it was that he had almost forgotten the contact whom he had been told to expect. There had been so many other things to remember during his short stay in the English countryside.

Not only did he spend hours doing exercises or leaping around a basketball court, not only did he have to cram the game's history and mechanics, outstanding matches and the names of famous players, but he also had to absorb what it was like to be an insurance salesman who lived in Hove.

All that remained in Apple's mind of basketball lore was that the tallest player ever was a Russian who scratched the wall at seven feet seven inches. The fact was bound to have stayed with Apple, despite not being particularly piquant: it was a comfort.

That his memory hadn't bothered to retain the player's name gave Apple comfort now, as well as reminding him of the matter of names. The next on his list of prospects was called Igor Kerensk.

The Soviet bus stopped in front of Harp Hall. It was greeted with cheers. There were hundreds of fans outside the stadium as well as the thousands waiting inside.

The Russian bus, one among several that were drawn up in the area reserved for teams, began unloading. Most of those getting out wore red blazers.

Fans edged closer. Some waved autograph books. Yes, Apple thought, going forward.

His search was made easy by there being only two males among the autograph hunters. He went to the youth and asked, "Remember me?"

"Yes, sir. I got you this morning. Thanks a lot, by the way."

"My pleasure," Apple said with subdued grandeur.

"I swapped you and a Schmidt for a Capelli."

Apple got straight to business, asking which among the newcomers was Igor Kerensk. The youth pointed him out. Moving on, Apple took sights on the tall man who looked as bleak as Siberia on a Sunday. He had solemn eyes, a pointed nose, a sullen mouth.

Kerensk had been sidling between his colleagues. Now he left them behind and went through the crowd, pace firm. When a reporter tried to intercept him, he brushed straight past.

Apple realised that he and his prospect were on convergent courses. They would meet in about one minute. It would look beautifully natural.

Apple scanned behind for a check on the Hammer and Sickle. Each was occupied. When Apple turned back, he had to jerk to a halt to avoid blundering into the man who had planted himself there and who said accusingly:

"I heard that you were sick on the airport bus."

"A foul lie."

"I should've been told about it. What?"

"A lie," Apple said. "I get travel sick only when I ride a bicycle."

The man hesitated, shook his head, said, "And now, at the hotel, I couldn't find you."

Apple began to hurry through an explanation. He was worried about losing Igor Kerensk.

The man looked sulky. Known as Whipper, he served the U.K. contingent in the rôle of bully, time-watcher and fink. He was average build, forty, and had a twitchy face.

"So I walked," Apple concluded. His eyes were fretfully on Igor, who was drawing away.

"Mr. Teever," Whipper said. "You might have the goodness to look at me when I talk to you."

Apple obligingly looked. He said, "I must be going."

"We all must. We're due on the court in ten minutes."

"Good." With a glance away he was just in time to see Igor moving out of sight between two buses.

Whipper, facetiously: "We don't want to be late, do we?"

"You know the answer to that," Apple said. It was the standard spook reply to what you hadn't heard properly or didn't want to waste your time on. "Excuse me." He went by swiftly.

Seconds later, he was turning between the same two buses. There was no sign of Igor. Hurrying, Apple went on to the rear of the vehicles, where he came to an abrupt stop.

Igor Kerensk was an instant too slow in tossing behind him the lighted cigarette.

Got you, Apple thought as he moved forward. He brought out a cigarette packet, which he opened and offered, grinning. Igor, sagging from his taut act of innocence, smiled gratefully. In silence they lit their cigarettes.

Apple began on his opener: "My name is John. I am being a student of languages. Will you mind if I talk at you in Russian? I desire to obtain the most practice."

While making the untidy yet true statement in respect of languages, Apple had looked Igor straight in the eye. Training Three said that if you did this when speaking a truth, your mark would instinctively know it to be so, and thereafter would tend to believe whatever else you said.

Igor Kerensk was saying in a friendly if not enthusiastic way that he would be happy to oblige: foreigners should be encouraged to learn the world's finest language.

Apple liked that, the blatant nationalism. It often meant the reverse.

After smoothing the way with the mention of a mother, Apple said that his father never discussed his professional life at home. "If he did, it would be interesting."

Igor Kerensk blew out smoke. "But fathers can be problems. For instance mine. He's got a good position, but he has a failing."

"What is it?"

"He's an idiot."

"Oh."

"For one thing, he has no faith in the new five-year plan for potato production. I won't bore you with other items."

"I see. You and he differ on official matters."

"I imagine so."

Apple shook his head. "I do not understand."

"I mean," Igor said, "that if we got together we'd no doubt hold opposing views on dozens of things, as in the past. We haven't exchanged a word in two years."

Apple, forlornly: "You haven't exchanged a word . . ."

"In two years," Igor said. He held up two fingers.

Straw-clutching: "Perhaps your father talks to your mother, and she talks to you."

"My mother died when I was born."

"Oh," Apple said. "I'm sorry."

The athlete tossed off a shrug. "That's history." He talked on. The subject was his idiot father, Apple heard distantly while condoling with himself for having struck lead again.

Dropping his cigarette, Igor said, "Thanks for the smoke. Maybe I can return the favour sometime."

They shook hands formally and the Russian left. Apple took one last, deep, consoling draw on his cigarette before throwing it away and going back into the thinning crowd.

He saw the girl. His neck clicked.

Clearly in view among the shorter people around her, the girl was coming in his direction. She scanned about like a meeter at a railway station.

Apple was still wondering about that when it ended. The girl's eyes settled. They settled on Apple himself. It seemed. He turned around to see who had been spotted. There was no one. He turned back.

Her gaze on his face, the tall girl came straight to Apple, halted neatly and cleared her throat. In awkward English with a poor accent she said:

"Excuse, please. My name is Dui Karpov. I am studying your language. Will you be inconvenienced if I did talk to you with briefness. I love to practice."

They stood looking at each other. Apple was busy being surprised/amused by the coincidence of what the girl had said, in addition to being impressed by the girl herself. Up close, she was far prettier.

"Wonderful," he said. "That you're learning English."

"I think that too."

"You speak it very well. I'll be happy to talk to you."

"You are extremely kind."

"My name's John Teever," Apple said. "I'm a player with the British outfit."

"Outfit?"

Apple began to explain. By his earnestness he realised that he was already smitten with this tall, tall girl.

Which, he thought sternly, was not a good idea. No benefit could come from having such an emotion for such a person. So being smitten had to be cancelled.

From past experience, however, Apple knew that he was wasting his time in trying to give himself orders. With a mental sigh, he submitted to the inevitable.

His lesson in idiomatic usage over, Apple passed on to the competition. He ended, "I'm only a reserve."

It seemed to make no difference. The girl said, "Myself, I am a masseuse. I stroke the bodies of the men."

Apple might have blushed except for being intrigued. The girl's profession had started all manner of sugar plums dancing in his head. He said, face straight, "That's an important job."

"True. I am in Dublin, however, through luck. The usual masseur took infirm, and I replaced him."

"All the luck is mine," Apple said boldly, bowing.

The girl smiled, showing small, even teeth like scalloped lace. "That is charming of you, John Teever."

"Just John will do. May I call you Dui?"

"Of course," she said, her smile widening.

All signs, Apple mused cheerfully, pointed to the fact that Dui's Russian emotions had reached a favourable decision about John Teever.

A bell rang loudly.

Both Apple and the girl said, "Oh dear." Then they laughed. There was more laughter when next they both started to talk of another meeting.

Apple said, "It can happen, can't it?"

"Yes, I hope so."

"How about this evening? If you can get away. Alone."

Dui said, "It might not be easy. They are inclined to be strict. Less so for me, however, than for the players."

"Then, you think you can manage it?"

"I believe I could be free at seven o'clock."

"Fabulous," Apple said. Noting that people were moving into the building, he started to speak quickly. "You know where O'Connell Street Bridge is, I'm sure. It's only a couple of minutes from your hotel."

"Yes, everyone knows the bridge. It is famous."

"How about if we meet on this side of it?"

"That will be perfect," Dui said. "But now we must part. Until later, John, at seven."

"Until later," Apple said with another bow.

The girl moved away. Apple watched her for a moment, drawing in a long, happy breath, before clicking into action. He strode toward one of the doors.

Presently, Apple was part of the organised throng. With banners and flags held high, a band playing as it led the way, and twelve thousand spectators cheering, the competing teams paraded into the court.

Apple thought about Dui.

While doing so, he scanned about to see if he could locate her. His view became blocked by the team alongside, the West Germans.

Switching from Dui to her colleagues, the mission in mind, which he considered efficient of him, Apple leaned toward the closest man and asked, in German, "Which one of you lot is called Ivan Ganin?"

The athlete said, "That name's out of the Soviet Union, not Germany."

"Well, could you point him out to me in the Red team?"

"Don't know him. Sorry."

That ended the exchange and Apple felt free to go back to thinking about Dui. He had not been idle.

With only minor mistakes, the teams finished up arranged into a horseshoe around the court. An official, comforting his lapels, closed with a microphone. The speeches were off and rambling.

Apple's group was still to the left of the German team, beyond whom came a patch of tall Swedes. Next to them were the Russians.

Apple started craning to try for a view of Dui. He had been doing this for some minutes, with poor results, when he felt a touch on his arm. Turning, he saw that one of the main British players had moved closer.

With a tentative smile, the man asked, as one bird-fancier to another, "Looking for that tall Commie dolly, eh?"

A known connexion with Dui not advisable as far as Apple was concerned, he answered in a cool manner, "I don't know what you mean."

The man eased away, his expression stating that he regretted his impulse to make a friendly overture. Apple could have trod on his own toes for his ill-conceived response. He tried to think of a healer; failed; gave up and went back to watching the Soviets.

By the time a third official was speeching, Apple had managed to get several glimpses of Dui, and once they had exchanged a smiling look. His smittenship was coming along.

Noting also Yek Milyukov and Igor Kerensk, the only Soviet players to whom he could put a name, Apple thought of the obvious healer for his colleague.

Turning back to the man, Apple asked with a smudge of humility, "I wonder if you'd be kind enough to tell me which is Ganin, in the Russian team there."

This not only gave an explanation for his rubber-necking, and flattered by suggesting that his colleague knew all the rivals, but it also stood a chance of bringing a needed answer. Apple was proud of the line.

But the man looked at him with one of those you-must-be-stupid expressions. He said, "First of all, Ivan Ganin isn't a player. He's a top-rank masseur."

"He is?"

"And second, he's not in the group over there. He's not even in Ireland. He never left Russia. He fell ill."

"Oh," Apple said. It was more sigh than word. The caper had died.

The first game of the play-offs started after the opening ceremony. Apple didn't stay around. Dui had left with the Soviet group, and he needed to be alone to do some drab thinking about the dead mission.

As he walked toward town from Harp Hall, however, Apple realised that no one but himself knew of the caper's death. Angus Watkin might, maybe, have heard by now of Ivan Ganin's absence, but he didn't know that Ganin, by a process of clever elimination, had been shown to be the right prospect. It could still be one of the other two, for all that Watkin was aware.

Therefore, Apple continued, thinking in Italian for the appropriate Machiavellian flavour, all he had to do in order not to be pulled out, which is what would happen if he told Angus Watkin the truth, was to keep quiet about his knowledge.

It wouldn't be like lying, Apple assured himself in Kremlin Russian, because he wouldn't be saying anything. He wouldn't be saying anything at all. There was no one to say anything to. He had no regular reports to make; had been told, in fact, to contact Upstairs only in an emergency.

Apple stopped walking. He straightened, smiled, sagged again on a nod.

Silence, he mused by visualising the matter in mutes' finger-language, would be the golden rule for the time being. He could stay on in Dublin. It wasn't a caper, but it almost had been. And there was Dui.

Apple walked on.

The tall Russian girl stayed in his mind; the girl as she looked and acted; only peripherally did he touch on the oddity of Dui's language-practice approach, the way she had gazed at him searchingly while introducing herself, and the fact of her being not only a replacement, but the replacement for Ivan Ganin.

Apple moved brightly in and out of daydreams about Dui during the following two hours, as he strolled admiringly around the city of Dublin.

Narrow streets twisted and turned like the politically adept or escaping outlaws. There were bookshops that out-quainted Dickens. Trinity College was stout-froth beige and morning-after green. Pubs ranged from the opulent to the hovelesque.

Aged between eight and eighty, beggars glared in warning, rather than gazed in supplication.

Apple returned to his hotel. After skirting a group of British players in the lobby, he went up to his room. The door was locked, there was no one inside, and not one article was even slightly out of place.

Yes indeed, Apple thought, the caper is dead.

He lay on the bed and dozed off. When he awoke, dusk was leaning on the windows. He snapped a look at his watch. It showed a quarter to seven. He would need to hurry.

As Apple got up, a knock sounded on the door. This bloody room, he thought, is jinxed.

He called out, "Who is it?"

"Whipper," a voice said. "Aren't you ready yet?" The door handle rattled.

"Ready?" Apple asked uneasily.

"Everyone else is downstairs, getting in the bus."

"I don't know what you're talking about."

Whipper said in a near-snarl, "Let's not have any nonsense." The handle rattled again. "Open up."

"I still don't know what you're talking about."

"The training session, man. The bus is taking us to the gymnasium. Has your watch stopped?"

Oddly, it had never occurred to Apple that he would actually have to do any playing or practicing. He said, "Yes, I know about the training session, and no, my watch has not stopped. But I can't go."

"Why not?"

Apple looked around the room in search of an excuse. He found none. He coughed. It was better than nothing.

The man outside said, "Open the door, Teever."

"I can't do that, either," Apple said, thinking about the

shrinking time left before the date with Dui. He pressed fingers to his brow to encourage other, interior action.

Whipper both rattled the handle and thumped the wood, saying, "This is all most peculiar, Teever. *Why* can't you open the door? *Why* can't you go to the session?"

An answer came to Apple. He had been inspired by the threat of his cover being blown from the inside, which would infuriate Angus Watkin.

"I'm shy," he said, yanking at the clothes on his upper body to get them off.

From outside came an incredulous, drawn-out, "You're shy?"

Always had been, from childhood, Apple explained while flinging off garments. When naked to the waist, he unlocked the door. He drew it six inches from the jamb and leaned across the space with his trunk. His lower half was hidden.

He said, "I've got no clothes on."

"So put some on."

"Can't. They've been pinched. Stolen. Every stitch I own. I don't even have a pair of underpants. I can't go either to the training session or anywhere else."

With his face twitching, Whipper said, "This is it. This is the bleeding limit."

"It's not my fault."

"No one said it was. I'm not talking about you."

Apple asked, "What's that?"

With a nod at the end of each sentence, Whipper grated, "The joke is over. Messing up a room is one thing. This is taking horseplay too far. This is interfering in serious matters. This is the end."

"Wait a minute," Apple protested, seeing the drift. "I'm not making any accusations. I've been robbed, that's all. People're always getting robbed in hotels."

But Whipper had stopped listening. He turned away, walked off and nodded himself out of sight along the hall, sentencing the team. Apple needed that, he reflected, like he needed a skin-lightener.

He closed the door. So that he wouldn't feel badly about the innocent being unfairly charged and convicted, he thought of the nuisance of all this, just when the team seemed willing to unfreeze.

Meanwhile, Apple hurried back into his clothes. He splashed water on his face, rumpled it part-dry, combed his hair, left the room, and went at a cautious speed down to the lobby.

The chartered bus, Apple could see, had gone. He also noted that no one connected with the United Kingdom sports entourage was present in the lobby. Reporters there were, in and close to the open-fronted bar, but they wouldn't be interested.

Crossing toward the hotel entrance, Apple saw that one of the reporters was Scoopsy. The hawk-faced American sat slouched in an armchair near the bar's front, a glass in one hand. He appeared to be dozing.

Apple covered the lobby and went outside. A light drizzle was falling from the night-dark sky. Many of the passers-by had umbrellas.

Across the way were three well-dressed women whose umbrellas were white placards. On catching sight of Apple, the trio, interrupting a smiling chat with the nearby policeman, lifted their placards vertical long enough for them to be read by the super-alert.

Apple blamed the weather for his failure to get the message. Signalling a thumbs-up agreement anyway, for the fellow-underdogness of it, he turned away.

As he went at a brisk walk through the lamp-lit streets, Apple reckoned that from this moment on he was safe in respect of

Whipper and the missing clothes. They, he would say, had been found under the bed, unstolen. That would solve his own small problem of explanation, although it wouldn't let the team off the hook.

Apple thought about it.

Again, inspired now by guilt, he came up with an answer. The diligent Whipper would be told that the clothing-hiding culprit had been unmasked. He was John Teever himself, who always did strange things if he walked in his sleep, which is what frequently happened when he was staying in hotels.

Pleased, the tail of blame pinned in the right place, Apple broke into a jog.

CHAPTER 3

Dui was there first. She stood out among the stream of pedestrians, most of whom gave her either a staring appraisal or a wide berth.

It wasn't often, Apple mused understandingly, that you saw a woman of that height, never mind the anachronism of her present garb.

Dui was wearing a bulky, ankle-length cloak with a hood, which was up. The colour was drama black. She looked like Anna Karenina waiting for a train to throw herself under, Apple thought. He agreed that the hood did help to keep her face hidden, but she was as noticeable as a missing nose.

With several passers-by having stopped, a group was in danger of forming by the time Apple arrived. He exchanged a brief greeting with Dui, took her elbow and walked her off. They went along beside the river. It murmured below them as smoothly as Guinness in a gizzard.

Apple, feeling like the hero of a Russian novel, was about to break the short silence when he was beaten to it by the explosion.

It was right behind them.

Releasing Dui's elbow, Apple whirled.

His first awareness was of normality: everything looked as it should. His second awareness was of causation: the old truck parked nearby, a man bent impatiently over its steering wheel, sounded ready to give another backfire.

Apple's third awareness was of Dui, at the same moment as she, obviously, was seeing him with a new awareness of her own.

Which led Apple to a fourth awareness.

He was still registering the fact that the Russian girl was crouched in the classical stance of unarmed combat, hands forward and flat, when he realised why she had her gaze on him so firmly.

Instinctively, he had fallen into that same stance himself. He was in it still.

A second backfire acted like a starting-pistol. Apple and Dui ended their tableau. With mumbles and small coughs, they began to straighten.

Dui turned to walk on. As Apple joined her she said, "That noise startled me somewhat."

"It startled me as well."

"I am not a city person."

"I live in a small town," Apple said. He was telling himself dazedly that a massage-expert would, of course, being involved with all manner of physical doings, know how to take care of herself properly. He added:

"The town's so small, in fact, that you could call it a village."

"It is the same with me."

"Good," Apple said inappropriately, his attention still divided. He wondered what Dui was thinking of his own display of spookcraft. Or was she wondering what he was wondering about hers?

On the heels of that came a question of more urgency. Ought he, with a casual manner, try to explain away his action, say he had taken up karate recently as a hobby?

"Er, look," Apple began, while Dui said at the same time, "Listen . . ."

They both gave short, humourless laughs and unisoned, "You first."

Politely, they both fell silent.

Apple hoped Dui would be telling herself that an athlete would, of course, know how to defend himself in a professional way. There was no reason why she should jump to the conclusion that he was a British espionage operative—which would have her running.

And that she was not doing, Apple thought. So the incident was best ignored. Trying for explanations could only make it worse, bigger.

He said, "There's this gym I go to."

Dui, being inside the hood and facing away, hadn't heard. She turned back with, "You know, I was talking to members of my team this afternoon."

There was a cautious note in her voice, Apple judged. He then realised precisely what Dui was going to bring up. And she did.

"Two of our players," Dui said, "made mention of being talked to by an English player called John. That must be you."

"Well, yes, I suppose it must," Apple said. He tutted mentally at his slowness. He should have seen sooner that the girl might hear about his chats to Yek Milyukov and Igor Kerensk.

Dui smiled. There was more of it in her eyes than on her lips. "So, John," she said, "you know a little of my language. That is wonderful. You should have told me."

"Well . . ."

"But possibly you were intending to give me a surprise at an opportune moment."

"Well . . ."

"Let me hear you say something in Russian, please."

The Russian that Apple used to explain about his recent

learn-by-post course was so bad that he felt proud of his nerve.
He switched to English to finish:

"If you don't mind, Dui, I'll stick to my native tongue. You
speak it so much better than I speak yours."

Nodding, Dui continued to talk in English—though she
threw in an occasional Russian phrase as if in encouragement.
Her family was the subject. She had a brother in the infantry
and a housewife sister; her mother was a secretary and her
father was a plumber.

These commented on, she asked, "What is the job of your
father, John?"

Apple wiped the rain from his face, slowly, to give reason to
his pause. He thought it odd that Dui should swoop straight to
the subject of parents and their professions. Could she be a go-
between for the man whose place she had taken in the Soviet
entourage?

"You are becoming wet without a coat," Dui said.

"I don't mind," Apple said, in truth, being hardly aware of the
weather. He was enjoying himself. The scene had romance, the
situation intrigue. All he lacked to make it perfect was a trench
coat.

"You asked about my father," he said. "He has a small business. A grocery shop."

Dui's step seemed to falter; but then she settled back into a
steady walk.

Apple: "He's not a big-shot. Yours isn't either, of course, but I
suppose you do know a lot of people who have important fathers."

Dui shook her hood. "No, I don't."

"Not one?"

"Not one. The only important people I am familiar with are

my superiors, in one way or another. The people who give me orders."

Apple digested that Dui was probably not a go-between after all for Ivan Ganin, while being distantly aware that her English seemed to have become less pedantic.

Dui looked at him. "I was sure," she said, "that I heard Yek mention that you'd told him something different."

"Different about what?"

"The profession of your father. Yek said that it was in aircraft designing."

"Dad retired from that and bought the shop."

Dui said a limp "Ah."

Apple thought about that while remembering everything else that had been said, along with Dui's stand-in status, her initial language-practice approach, her searching look at that time, her reaction to the truck's backfire, her rapidly improving English.

The last struck Apple as convenient. He decided to use it as a trap.

Being as sloppy in diction as he could, and putting a hand near his mouth to further dull clarity, he said, "I'd give a coupla limbs for a coffin-nail." Dui's knowledge of English, he mused, would have to be perfect for her to catch and tame that one.

She mumbled off-handedly, "Don't smoke, myself."

Then her hood went up as she straightened, which is what Apple was doing himself as he pulled the evidence together. He was only semi-conscious of answering when now Dui spoke again; but came alert on realising that he had replied in Russian with an affirmative to Dui's question, posed in the same language:

"Are you cognizant of the deleterious consequences upon diverse locations of the anatomy from pulmonary ingestion of nicotine?"

Apple and Dui stopped walking. They turned to face one another. It was that post-backfire moment again. But this time its life was briefer.

Before Apple could decide whether or not to try to divert mental attention by informing that the word *nicotine* came from a Jean Nicot, who introduced tobacco into France in 1560, he was joining Dui in looking back between them.

Their focus was the same: the car that had just come to a halt.

"The espionage game of follow-my-leader differs from the children's version insofar as you can finish up playing dead for real." Thus an instructor in Training Three. "If, then, a person or vehicle stops when you do, think the worst."

The car stood fifty feet back. It was on the other side of the road and some way out from the kerb. Rain as well as poor street lighting allowed only a suggestion of the plain vehicle with its driver and one rear-seat passenger.

The eyes of Dui and Apple met again. Apple, hoping his expression was as non-committal as hers, asked, "Shall we give it another chance?"

She nodded. "Good idea."

They faced front and walked on. After a pause, Apple heard the car creak and hum into movement. In a conversational tone he said:

"There's a foot-bridge further along. It crosses the Liffey. We can split up there if we're being tailed. You take the bridge, I'll play lead for the car."

Dui asked, "You're the guy in the white hat, eh?"

"I refuse to let a lady draw the shadow."

"I adore chivalry."

"But maybe they're friends of yours."

"It's more likely they're your friends. This is home territory for you."

"Don't let an Irishman hear you say that."

Dui pointed ahead. "Is that the foot-bridge?"

"Yes," Apple said. "And if we do have to split up, let's meet again later. Say in an hour."

Dui said, "I can't stay away that long. But what I could do is this: go back to the hotel and leave again after a while. The longer I stay there, visibly, the better. Let's call it ten o'clock."

She agreed to Apple's suggestion of meeting place, the Sober Tinker, a pub on the other side of the river. As all along during this exchange, Apple spoke flowing Russian and Dui talked in fluent English.

"All right," Apple said. "Now we test the car."

They came to a natural-seeming stop. Their coordination was so good, they might have been practicing for an hour. They didn't look back.

The car behind also halted. Apple knew this by a fast reduction in the sounds he had been listening to and a change to stillness of the headlight beam he had been watching.

Dui said, "Yes."

Apple said, "Right."

They walked on. The car followed. They covered the final yards to the bridge, where they separated. Dui turned off between the wrought-iron railings; Apple kept walking. Neither one broke step.

Apple quickened his step. He still had part of his attention on the car's lights and sound. He was aware at once when they changed. He looked back.

The car was crawling as it drew level with the foot-bridge. The impression given was one of indecision. It ended with the car coming forward again.

Apple strode on.

He realised why he hadn't suggested to Dui that they meet as soon as he had shaken the shadow; he needed time to cogitate on what the signs foretold.

Which was that Dui Karpov had to be a Sickle.

Those bits of business, from a close look in the listener's eyes while telling a truth, to that backfire reaction, all pointed to Dui being a trained KGB agent.

And, Apple further thought, he, too, was giving out signs (all no doubt duly read by Dui) that he was an espionage operative also.

Apple would have liked to be able to ask his team colleagues if they had been approached by Dui with the language-practice bit (and he thought he had been so original with that), but it wasn't possible on account of frosty relations.

Stepping off the kerb, Apple set out across the roadway. He went at an oblique angle, not straight, in order to make the crossing last as long as possible.

Apple was unsure about the situation with Dui. To change that, he would have to find out if she was definitely KGB or if those signs were merely coincidental/circumstantial. But how would he go about establishing one or the other?

Ignoring a faint tingle of disappointment because the tail car hadn't come speeding at him over the water-glistening, lamp-lit tarmac, Apple reached the opposite side of the road.

He turned into a side street. It had a scattering of pedestrians who were hurrying to dryness, one or two moving vehicles.

What the people following him were up to, and why, Apple had no notion. There were many possibilities, ranging from the lethal to the innocuous. But, at the moment, he was more interested in Dui Karpov.

There was one quick way, Apple thought, to try to find out if

Dui was a Sickle. Bluff. That would do the trick. He could tell her that her cover had been blown.

Which, of course, Apple realised, would mean the blowing of his own cover. It would state as clearly as a confession that he was a spook himself. Since this was a non-caper, however, it wouldn't really matter.

Apple got another idea. It was one that would allow him to stay inside John Teever, keep the enjoyable mask in place.

Dui only suspected him of being a Brit, Apple mused. So what if he were to fake himself off to her as straight, and then, after hinting up to it cautiously, say that he had classified material to sell?

That, Apple agreed, would help romance like nothing else could. What, in fact, would a female agent *not* do to push an espionage mission along to success?

Apple dwelled on that.

He would have slipped into erotic reveries, with ease, except for being slightly more enthralled by the sinister cunning of his idea. He almost snickered, which made him uneasy, and returned him to normalcy.

Apple gave his head a short, curt shake.

There would be no leading of young maidens up the garden path, he thought sternly. It wasn't honest. And with him being smitten, more now than before, it would be ten times worse. The idea was out; a bluff was in.

Apple realised that he was getting more than just damp. If it weren't for that, he would have happily gone on like this for ever, or at least until it was time to go to the Sober Tinker.

At the next corner he came to, Apple turned off. Here there were more people about, but no one who could serve his slip-giving purpose. He went on to the next corner. Once around it, he saw a couple who would do.

The older man and woman were going straight on, about to cross to the other side of the junction. Apple joined them on the far side, at the same time losing a foot in height by sinking at the knees.

He was half-way across the road, and still making up a trio, before the woman of the pair looked around at him, and before the tail car came along to make the turn.

The woman smiled in doubt. She wasn't sure about this. She became less so when her eyes flicked down to the bent legs.

But Apple was on his way. He moved ahead in order to put the useful couple between himself and the car, which was now turning in the direction he had been taking. The old routine had worked.

Apple straightened to his full height as he stepped over the kerb. The tailing intrigue was finished, but he was gratefully recalling that he had actually had that cunning idea. It showed that there might, after all, be something fascinating and malign stirring in the depths of his being.

Although, Apple thought in an attempt at toning it down, the idea hadn't been all that weird. And even if it had, surely he deserved some excess as consolation for having been sent to Dublin on a fools-rush.

Apple turned into a down-sloping street. Conveniently, it went toward the river, which winked at lights in the near distance.

Only half a dozen strides had he taken when the rain, ending its playfulness, began to come down like a pro. Apple sprinted to the doorway of a dingy shop, thinking: taxi.

The street, two-lane narrow, was brightly lit and with constant traffic. But the screen of rain blurred images. Apple had to run out of his shelter whenever he saw a vehicle that resembled a taxicab.

After having done this several times, getting steadily wetter, he spotted another prospect and again darted out to the kerb, arms waving.

A taxi it was; but it bore a full complement of passengers. They, Apple saw, as at the same moment they recognised him, were team colleagues.

Apple stopped waving and dropped his arms. Raising theirs, while smiling in dry smugness, the non-playing members of the British entourage waved.

When the taxi passed, Apple went at a grumpy run across the road, heading for a dilapidated pub. He needed it as much for its merchandise as for shelter. A drink would help him forget that he had wanted to thumb his nose.

Inside, the pub was warm and pink, like a puppy's belly. It had a dozen customers. There was no one under fifty and the sole woman had passed that mark twenty years before.

They were too involved in their conversations to pay the tall stranger much heed. While ordering a drink, Apple picked up that one topic was religion, one politics, and a third religious politicians. Also, that the shawl-draped woman was talking about the violets she had sold today from the empty basket at her feet.

His hot toddy—lemon, sugar, boiling water and Irish whiskey —was served to Apple absently: the gnarled landlord had his attention on the flower-seller's saga, which was proceeding bunch by bunch.

Apple stood with his back to the bar. He sipped his comforting drink and enjoyed the local colour. Listening all around, he nodded agreements, pursed his lips in doubt, pulled for a sale when the old woman told of a near-miss.

Gradually, talk faded. Soon only the saga was being unfolded; and that ended when a man whispered in the flower-seller's ear.

There had, Apple recalled, been quite a bit of whispering going on previous to the close of conversation. He supposed, blasély, that everyone was just realising that present was one of the visiting basketball top-liners.

And true enough, the customers were now looking at him, Apple saw, though they had a furtiveness that he found odd. Which oddness increased as the landlord sidled out from behind his bar to join the lookers.

The room was silent, still.

No longer blasé, Apple turned with a growing uneasiness from face to face. The expressions on display were either grim or inscrutable. In no way did they suggest interest in a sports personage.

Could be, Apple mused, that he had innocently done the wrong thing; or that the people were anti-competition; or that they were mistaking him for one of the other foreign visitors, some player who had been in here and created a bad scene.

Apple tensed. This was because the seated customers—two men and the flower-seller—were slowly rising from their chairs; and, strangely, doing so without taking their fixed gazes off the tall stranger.

Apple tensed still more, once the ex-sitters were erect. This time it was because he had the impression, ridiculous though it may be, that the people were beginning to edge toward him.

Head still, Apple sent his eyes to their corners in order to check on the crescent of people. His impression, he saw with astonishment, was sound.

The people, landlord and flower-seller included, were moving forward at a deliberate creep. Not only that, but most of them had stooped into the predator's crouch.

Apple tried a laugh. It came out as a dry cackle, like a bill leaving its envelope.

Taking a grip on himself, Apple decided that he must be hallucinating. This was too incredible to be real. Could the hot toddy been topped up with a drug?

Apple put his glass on the counter. On turning back, he saw that the people had stretched their hands out. Their pace was faster, their faces were determined, their eyes gleamed excitement.

No, Apple thought, he hadn't been drugged, it was no hallucination.

"You know," he said, his voice with a puberty break in it, "I've never been in this charming place before."

At which point, small hell broke out.

With a sudden rush, shattering the pub's quiet with shouts, the people swooped. They converged on Apple like buyers on a bargain.

He gulped in alarm. But no blows landed. That helped. It held his alarm at a steady pitch. He offered little resistance as he was grabbed by his arms and clothing and pulled away from the bar.

In any case, Apple was afraid of hurting his older antagonists, not one of whom reached his shoulder. Even if he simply leapt forward, he would unavoidably knock over the flower-seller, who was towing him by his tie, panting.

Apple, struggling feebly, remembered that he had a voice. He asked, loudly, "What's going on? What've I done?" He was ignored.

Someone opened the door. The group manhandled Apple over to it. He steeled himself for the shove that would send him flying outside.

It didn't happen. Instead, the people surged out into the rain with him. They were still shouting.

Those shouts. For the most part, they were instructional in nature, with everyone telling everyone else what to do. In between, however, there were snatches of talk that seemed to tell a story.

The people bundled their captive down the sloping street, hurrying now. Their shouts also had greater urgency. But the mood was low on animosity. It was as if the important thing were to keep the stranger moving.

While he continued his struggle to free himself without hurting anyone, Apple was listening to the snatches of talk that came between shouts. And while he protested his innocence of whatever he was thought guilty of, he was busy putting those snatches together.

By the time he had been manhandled half-way along the street, Apple knew the first section of the story.

The landlord had been telephoned by the Irish Republican Army. A tall, pale, freckled member of the IRA, drunk, had made off with a bomb. It was of the new, stationary type, invented to prevent accidents in transit. Settled, motionless, it could explode, but was safe as long as it was moving; or, as with most bombs, wet.

The middle section of the story, Apple worked out for himself. His taxi-riding colleagues were responsible. They wanted him out in the rain again. Their telephoned story, though absurd, was one which nobody in bomb-conscious Ireland could afford to disregard.

The story's last section Apple got when it was too late to change the ending. He was at the end of the street and being propelled at speed toward the river when he realised that his captors intended to make a thorough job of wetting the bomb.

Loudly, he denied being in possession of any infernal machines. Again he was ignored. Firmly, he tried to free himself. Again this proved impossible without the use of violence.

And then he was against the parapet, above which he towered. The flower-seller, having made a sprightly leap out of the way, yelled, "Over with him!"

He went over.

As he headed for the water, Apple, resigned, was telling himself that, as he would now have to bathe and change, it was shrewd of him to have set the date with Dui for much later.

The Sober Tinker, with potted palms and fringed carpets, was the kind of pub where religion was never mentioned, politics was a dirty word, and the IRA was referred to like one of Mrs. Gershwin's lads.

Apple had been standing at the bar long enough to eat a couple of meat pies. He had also worked out how he was going to tell Dui that her cover had been blown. To give the simple statement more force and verity, he would present it with sympathy, rather than scoff or hardness.

Dui came in as the clock was striking. She still wore her flamboyant cape. Its dryness showed that, like Apple, she had come by taxi.

A striking figure, Dui caused a mild sensation as she moved to the bar, where she put her hood down.

They spoke English during subdued greetings and while Apple got the drinks—sherry on the rocks for himself, gin and tonic for Dui. Public interest in them had faded by the time they had settled at a corner table.

They sipped, put down their glasses, and both began to talk at once, still in English. They broke off.

Apple said, "After you."

Dui nodded. She eased forward, smiled sympathetically and said, "Your cover's been blown."

Slowly, slowly, Apple leaned back in his seat. He was stunned and irked. He had been taken in as well as beaten to the draw. But it was his own fault. He ought to have known what Dui really was.

From her using the same approach as he had used, among other signs, not forgetting height, Apple thought, he should have realised sooner that Dui was the same as himself: a faceless one. And as such she would tend to think the same way he did. But at least, because of that, he hadn't fallen for the bluff.

Apple said, "This is what comes from being polite and letting a lady go first."

"Didn't you hear what I said?" Dui asked. Her expression was still sympathetic.

"Yes, and if my cover's blown, so is yours. You'd have to be a Sickle to know about it."

"Why couldn't the KGB tell me the result of their check on this unknown substitute?"

"For the simple reason that there is no result. My cover has *not* been blown."

"But you must be a Brit to know what a Sickle is."

Apple smiled. "No more bluffs?"

Dui, her acted sympathy gone, returned the smile with a nice naturalness. "It's a deal."

"And my cover, for your information, though feeble, is good for several weeks."

"So is mine."

They raised their glasses, clinked them together, sipped. Apple said, "I would not, of course, be talking to you like this if I weren't on a fools-rush. I suspect you are too."

"I wouldn't know about that," Dui said, "not knowing what the hell a fools-rush is."

"The reference is from fools rushing in where angels fear to tread."

"I think I see."

"The control uses an amateur who disobeys all the rules but sometimes, through luck or stupidity, wins out, where the pros would fail. His innocence is his greatest asset."

"Yes," Dui said. "Like the Finn last year who strolled into a certain building in Moscow and lifted some fairly important papers. A pro would never have thought to try it."

"Right. And equally important, the pro counter-spooks would never have expected it."

Dui asked, "You think we're both on a fools-rush?"

Apple nodded. He realised he ought to have recognised the form far earlier. That initial pick-up by Albert had been slip-shod; contact-man Malone was himself an amateur, one who blithely carried around an important number on paper instead of in his head; there was the lack of back-up.

"Well," Dui said, "I don't know if I like having the gods play games with us little people down here."

"If it's any consolation," Apple said, "I've been on these deals before and lived to tell the tale. Though I've never told it to anyone as attractive as you."

Dui smiled warmly. "Thank you, John. How sweet! Here's mud in your eye."

"Cheers."

They drank. Dui drained the glass with a gusto that filled Apple with admiration. He fetched another gin for Dui, and got himself a drink that looked the same but contained only tonic. Sole motive for this was to avoid having to explain that he had a low tolerance for alcohol.

Dui declined a cigarette. Watching Apple light up, she asked, "Why are we here in Dublin at all, at all?"

"I'm chasing a rumour, supposedly," Apple said. He blew out smoke in, he hoped, a gusto-like way. "A member of a foreign team might want to sell info. Sound familiar?"

"I'll say. It's the pitch I got. Is the info said to come from the player's father, who has a high position?"

"Exactly. It's the same story. Who got it first I don't know, but it looks as if our controls have been pushing it at each other, possibly for laughs."

"However," Dui said, "they couldn't risk ignoring it."

Apple shook his head. "I may be wrong, but if it had been sound, all you'd need is an experienced contact-maker. All this substitute stuff is to blind us underlings."

"It's that important?"

"If a man realises he's on a fools-rush, theory says, he starts to think and act differently. Which is destructive. It can also be fatal."

Dui said, "So we're expected to blunder around and hopefully happen to come up with something?"

"The gods have nothing to lose."

"Except us."

"We're replaceable."

"Well, the rumour does seem dead," Dui said. "There's no info-seller on the U.K. team, as far as I'm concerned."

"Same with me and your lot," Apple said. "Unless you, Ms. Karpov, would care to sell me a blueprint or two."

"Kind of you to ask. But I don't go in for the disloyalty bit myself."

"Me neither. It's so old hat."

Dui raised her glass and leaned back. She said, "Then, that's the end of the mission."

"Looks like it."

"Now what do we do—tell the gods our problems?"

"I don't much care for that."

"What we could do is relax and enjoy our paid holiday."

His tone and smile meaningful, Apple said, "That sounds like a wonderful idea."

Dui's smile had the same flavour, even though she said, "Yes, but there's two things we ought to do."

Apple, who had mainly one thing in mind, suggested, "Prevent ourselves from being pulled out?"

"Right. And the other thing is to get our own back, in a way, by grabbing some benefit from this fools-rush."

"Of course," Apple purred.

Patting his hand, Dui said demurely, "I meant career, not personal."

With a different interest: "Career?"

"What's good enough for the goose, as the proverb goes. We have the moral right to give ourselves a shove up the ladder."

"I buy it," Apple said. "But how do we go about it?"

"I thought you'd have scores of ideas."

"At this moment I'm not in a particularly inventive mood. However, I'm sure there must be plenty of schemes that'd work."

"I'm sure of it as well. Between us we'll come up with something. Meanwhile, here's to us."

"Us and success."

After taking a healthy draft of her gin and tonic, Dui said, "I'll be leaving soon. I think we should be careful."

"Right. We can't be seen too often together. But we'll arrange something."

"Talking of being seen. I hate to be nosy, but could you tell me who the shadows, earlier, were?"

"I truly could not," Apple said. "I hoped you might have a clue on that." When Dui shook her head, he went on to tell how he had given the car the slip. He spoke in the lazy way of someone who did that kind of thing all the time. The pub-river aftermath he failed to mention.

From there the talk became non-spook. Apple would have liked to ask Dui about her service background, but felt they had an unspoken agreement not to probe into things professional. It was rare enough that they had reached an understanding. Theirs, then, would be a personal relationship. That suited Apple fine.

With their third drink, which they agreed to make the last, they got back on the subject of safety. Dui said she thought they ought to leave separately. After agreeing reluctantly, Apple said:

"And there's the matter of us staying in the caper."

"Which means, of course, that we have to be making some kind of progress."

"I don't know how we're going to manage that one."

"I have an idea, as a matter of fact," Dui said. "We could each say that we'd made prelim contact with the other, and there might be info in the offing."

"Even though," Apple asked, doubtful, "the rumour seems to be false?"

"Right. And garnish with whatever frills are necessary."

"Frills need to be seen. Simply *saying* we've got a bite isn't going to go over big."

Dui nodded, smiling. "Then, we need to have observers see an exchange of signals between us."

Warming to the idea, which, in respect of the Porter-watcher, would give a legitimate excuse for meetings with Dui, and which would do the same for her in regard to her KGB colleagues, Apple said:

"Listen. Are you going to be at the Soviet-French game in the morning?"

"Yes. I have to be."

"I can be there as well. We'll do observable signals in the stadium, at different times."

"That's a fabulous idea, John. Let's play with some ideas for signals."

Leaning forward over the table, they put their heads together like a couple of spies.

Apple went into the street telephone booth. As habitual, he kept the door open with one foot to leave undisturbed his slumbering claustrophobia. He read the international operating directions carefully.

Coin slot fed, Apple dialled a series of numbers. The last section of these caused a particular telephone to ring somewhere in London. Although Apple had called the number often, he had no idea where the Upstairs building was located.

A man answered with a casual "Yes?"

Choosing a name at random, Apple said, "I'd like to speak with Mrs. Harvest."

The man said, "I think you've made a mistake. What number did you dial?"

Apple quoted six digits. The first three belonged to himself, the rest to the person with whom he wanted to talk. After a pause the man came back.

He said matter-of-factly, "Yes, you made a mistake." The line went dead.

So dear old Angus wasn't available, Apple mused as he put the receiver down. And Angus had to know about this beforehand, otherwise the whole thing would be pointless. The charade of signals had to be witnessed and reported on.

About to leave the booth, Apple recalled Malone. He was fast in putting a call through to the number he had memorised. A familiar voice answered.

Malone asked a laconic "Yes?"

They all love to play it cool, Apple thought. He said, "I'll assume that you know who I am, and get straight to the point. Okay?" His tone was news-reader with a hot one.

"Sure. Go ahead."

"Something's developed. I need to talk to someone from regions above the ground floor. Is there anybody of that nature around?"

"Well," the big Irishman said, producing the word as though it were helping him to lift a weight, "that depends on the importance of the development."

"It's vital enough for me to want to go as high as I can," Apple said. "That should give you the picture."

"Might take a while. Can I call you back? Are you at the hotel?"

"No, but call me there. It's safe enough if we keep it simple."

"Right," Malone said. "Over and out."

Apple left the booth, breathed deeply of the great outdoors and set off at a jog. As he had been half-way to his hotel before finding a vacant telephone box, he covered the rest of the journey in minutes.

He had towelled and recombed his hair by the time the telephone purred. As he came out of the bathroom to go to the instrument, a knock sounded briskly on the door.

Apple stopped. He called, "Who is it?"

There was no answer—except for a repeat of the knock. The telephone went on with its discreet purring. Apple again called to the knocker to identify himself. Again another knock was the only answer.

Stepping to the telephone, Apple lifted its receiver. He heard Malone's voice and told him to hold on. With the hand-set laid on the bedside table, he moved aside to the door, which he opened to a circumspect ajarness. This gap he didn't change on seeing the American reporter outside.

"Hi," Scoopsy said, smiling like an innocent child who knows there's no such thing as an innocent child. "How are you to-day?"

Apple grunted, "Fine."

"Sorry I didn't answer you, but sometimes people won't open up if they know it's the press. God knows why."

"But he's not telling."

Scoopsy shrugged. He said, "I hope I'm interrupting an intriguing telephone call, perhaps from a certain lady."

Apple said, "That was a message from the desk."

Peering inside: "Still is. The receiver's off."

"That's to guarantee peace. I'm going to bed. It's been fun talking to you here in downtown Dublin. Good night."

"Wait a mo. I want to know about you having had all your clothes stolen."

"It was a mistake."

"Did you borrow some? Why haven't you made a complaint to the hotel management? Which police officer is handling the case? Could I get a pic of you and the empty closet?"

"Negative to all questions," Apple said. "I found my clothes under the bed, where I'd put them myself, in my sleep."

Scoopsy looked sceptical. "Yeah?"

"Really and truly. I always do cuckoo things when I stay in a room that's not my own."

"Are you sure your clothes weren't pinched by a rival, romantic or sports?"

"Quite sure," Apple said. "And now, good night." He closed

the door firmly, didn't move away, and opened it again after half a minute. The reporter had gone.

Recovering the telephone receiver, Apple said, "Shoot."

Malone said, "I heard that exchange."

"Good. But I'd just like to know what's happening, if you don't mind."

"Okay. Here it is. And you'll need to act at once. Leave the hotel and turn left. Good night."

"Hey!" Apple said. "Hold on."

"Well?"

"Is that all? Walk to the left outside?"

"That's it," Malone said. "Good night." The line clicked to silence.

Replacing the receiver in its cradle, Apple told himself that, after all, that was all he wanted. The routine seemed straightforward enough. An agent, once having made sure from a safe distance that the scene was clean, would fall into step beside the lone walker.

Apple left the room, taking along a folding umbrella. One minute later he was entering the lobby. The first person he saw there, and who saw him, was Whipper.

The team scourge looked Apple up and down repeatedly like a tailor while walking toward him. They stopped when close. Whipper said he demanded an explanation.

"About what?"

"The stolen clothes, man, for God's sake."

"Ah yes," Apple said. He began elaborating on what he had told Scoopsy. As he did so, he noticed that two of the British star players were approaching. His gaze and theirs made contact. Apple gave an affable nod. The two men looked away; and stayed like that until they were out of sight.

Whipper, then, had already read the riot act, Apple thought.

He finished his explanation and nailed it home with "You know how these things are."

"No," Whipper said, "I don't." His face twitched. "I've never heard of it. Sleepstealing?"

"Very common among the honest," Apple said. "But let's not go into the psychology of it right now."

Whipper changed to a hard stare. "No, Teever, let's go into the possibility of you having made this up."

Apple put on the stark face of astonishment. "Made it up? Why would I do that?"

"To take the heat off the others, of course. You lot're hand in glove."

"You must be joking. The others don't even like me. It's the truth I'm telling you. In fact, that's why I'm going outdoors now."

"What d'you mean?"

"I'm going to walk and walk, tire myself out. Otherwise I might get up in my sleep. I might start breaking into other people's rooms."

"You might . . . ?"

"Exactly," Apple said, aware of the passing seconds. He went on glibly, "Thank you, by the way, for keeping a tight hold on things here. We'd be lost without you. If there's one person who really matters in this group, it's yourself." He nodded. "Good-bye for now, old man."

Leaving Whipper looking more than ever like a tailor, one who has put the sleeves on upside down, Apple went over to the main door.

Outside, he opened and raised his umbrella before setting off in the rain—to his left. There were no pedestrians, no moving vehicles, and the anti-British picketers were absent. In Dublin, most night-life ends when the pubs close.

Apple's guilt over the team being blamed for the clothing debacle helped him ignore the fact that he was under an umbrella. Such an item, in Apple's vista of espionage, was as acceptable to a spook as would be boots to a ballerina.

But the worst thing that could happen to him at present, Apple had realised, was a cold, entirely possible after that river incident. Runny eyes and noses were greater destroyers of budding romance than mutual hate.

Now Apple dismissed guilt and umbrellas, colds and romance, on realising that a car was coming along behind.

Not another one, he thought, or even the same one as last time. What were the stupid biblical-sensers up to?

Apple thought thus more in hope than resignation. He didn't really believe that he was the reason for the car's presence—as announced by lights and sounds. Coincidence had brought it, he knew, and any of a hundred reasons could explain its walking-speed slowness.

Apple had still not looked around. Nor did he do so now, not noticeably, as the vehicle's front came abreast and into his vision. He simply put on speed, striding out at a good clip.

The car fell behind. After a noisy change of gear, it came on anew.

The headlights threw Apple's shadow into a long, nightmare version of the tall reality. He was glad when the shadow zoomed off to one side, even though this meant that the car was once more drawing level.

Apple left it by breaking into a trot. His manner he maintained neat, proper. He ran with back straight, chin high, and umbrella held rigidly aloft.

Again the car came forward. This time, when its nose was

coming alongside, from the interior floated a voice to tear at the street's quiet:

"Would you stand bloody still a minute?"

Apple looked round as he slowed, verifying that the voice was indeed that of someone he knew. He and the vehicle came to a stop at the same time.

The man with white hair leaned through the window. He asked, "What's your hurry, Tom Thumb?"

Pleased at being unsurprised, Apple said, "I don't know if we've been introduced."

But Albert, patently, was in no mood for banter. His response was to direct a hooked thumb toward the back seat.

While putting down his umbrella and entering the car, Apple was forced to allow that if he were Albert he, too, would be disgruntled. The older man enjoyed as much as anyone else the chance to be in covert action. When you've been looking forward to bringing off a smooth pick-up, you don't like having it ruined by some lunatic who wants to play catch-me.

Albert stayed silent as he drove. That was fine with Apple, who, while mulling the situation over, was appreciating the turns the driver made to confound tails. Once, Apple looked behind; the road was void of traffic, but he understood.

On approaching a corner on a commercial street, the car slowed. It stopped at the kerb. With an index finger, Albert directed Apple's attention toward the mouth of a covered passageway. Within it, in shadow, stood the figure of a man.

Apple asked, "Journey's end?"

"Good-bye," Albert said, killing motor and lights.

Apple got out. He went into the passageway's darkness and stopped with a respectful sway beside the man, who greeted bleakly, "Porter."

Apple took the same line with "Sir." He had already digested the news that Angus Watkin was here in Dublin, which news had been given to him by the fact of Albert's presence.

"There is an emergency, Porter?" Watkin droned.

"Not quite, sir, no. But something's come up and I'd like your advice."

"*Invaluable* advice, Porter. If you use flattery, always make a thorough job of it."

"Well . . ."

"But it's past my bed-time. I would like to suggest that you make haste."

"Yes, sir," Apple said. "I think I should tell you first, however, that I was followed earlier this evening, by two men in a car." He reckoned it best to mention the incident in case there had been an observer.

"Give me details. Rapidly."

Apple began to do so. Accustomed by now to the gloom, he could see his control's face clearly. Which meant that his own features were clear to Angus Watkin.

Therefore Apple held his eyes in readiness to avert. This would be done downwards, not sideways: down used the eyelid, which was eight times faster than the eyeball.

"If you wish to worry about being followed," Angus Watkin said when Apple had finished, "feel at liberty to do it. What you describe is meaningless to me."

"Maybe they were straight, sir."

"Would you mind if we left your adventures, Porter, and got to the point of this pointless-seeming rendezvous?"

Apple straightened like a good underling, sagged again to a lower level than before so as not to tower over his control, and said with gaze averted:

"The situation is this, sir. One of our three prospects isn't here in Ireland. He took ill and had to stay in Russia. I've made contact with the other two, and they are definitely straight. So it looks as though the man named by that rumour is the one who's not in Dublin."

Angus Watkin nearly raised his eyebrows. "That, then, would appear to signify that your mission has come to an end."

"Except, sir," Apple said, looking down, "that the missing man's replacement, by a useful coincidence, seems to be interested in what I'm after."

"Indeed?"

"Yes, sir. She hinted that—"

"*She,* Porter?"

"A masseuse called Dui Karpov," Apple said. "She's gangly and rather plain."

"Pray continue."

"The young lady hinted at information to which she has total access."

"Information of which type, Porter?"

"That wasn't entered into," Apple said craftily. "Though she did drop in a casual way that her cousin is with the Moscow Institute of Technology."

After a pause, one which, Apple felt, had not come from his chief's pause repertoire, those acted gaps ranging from the deplete to the pregnant, Angus Watkin murmured, "How interesting!"

"We were both cautious," Apple said. "We weren't rushing into anything. In fact, we left it that if she's willing to go further with this business, she'll advise me to that effect tomorrow morning."

"By what means?"

"Physical signal, sir, at Harp Hall, at the French and Soviet game. It's tomorrow morning."

"So you just stated."

"And what I want to know is, do I press ahead with this development?"

Angus Watkin sniffed. He said, "Tell me, Porter, what is your own feeling?"

This was soft ground. Although Apple knew that his control couldn't afford to let the Dui-info possibility go unexplored, he also knew that Watkin would rather give an order than agree to a suggestion. Therefore he said:

"It seems a slim hope to me, sir, that this Karpov woman will come up with something useful."

"Speaking," Watkin said, "from your experience in these matters." Which, Apple knew, was the same as calling him a simpleton, since his experience was severely limited.

"Quite, sir," Apple said, the while blinking as though he had been praised.

Angus Watkin nodded slowly—and Apple's spirits held their breath. He wondered if, not for the first time, he had managed to out-clever himself. His control could now decide to bring in the contact expert he would have used in the first place, had the rumour been good.

Angus Watkin stopped nodding. This, Apple saw with a glance aside, was because a soft-footed couple had stopped by the passageway's mouth. They seemed to be on the verge of entering; but then they went on.

Watkin had gone back to the slow nods. Apple's spirits were bloated. They started breathing again, however, when, on a final nod, Angus Watkin said:

"I suppose, Porter, that it might be better if you stayed with it."

"Very good, sir."

"Nothing ventured, and so forth. It could be worth a snippet or two."

Apple, pushing: "Then, I was right to ask for this meeting, wasn't I, sir?"

"More or less. You could, of course, have used your own judgment. But no, you acted correctly."

Considering the weather and the hour and the lack of emergency, his chief, Apple mused, was being extremely pleasant. "Thank you, sir."

"To avoid further face-to-faces in damp alleys with inelegant smells, Porter, I shall give you a telephone number."

Now, that's the real-life, odious Watkin, Apple thought in vague relief. He offers a phone number as though it's the combination of an Upstairs safe.

"I appreciate that, sir."

"Ready to absorb?"

Number securely memorised, Apple said, "I shall report regularly on progress, sir."

"But spare me the blow-by-blow material, please. I want to hear about ends, not means."

Apple took a stooping, underling-style step to his rear. "Of course, sir," he said ingratiatingly. "Just as you say. You may rely on me."

Angus Watkin gave one of his sighs. He said, "Yes."

Turning to leave: "Good night, sir."

"Not so precipitous, Porter. Haven't you forgotten something?"

Apple looked around. "What, sir?"

"The physical signal. The one which will be transmitted to you tomorrow morning, at Harp Hall, by a young lady who is gangly and plain."

"Ah yes."

"What, Porter, is the signal?"

Apple related that Dui Karpov would appear in the stadium

with a towel around her neck. Once she had settled on the Russian team's bench at courtside, she would convey her affirmation by placing the towel over her head like a cowl.

"Thank you," Angus Watkin said. "Good night."

"Good night, sir," Apple said, turning away. He went out into the street and began putting up his umbrella as he walked. He was thoughtful.

CHAPTER 4

An air of excitement thrived in the stadium. It embraced Apple as soon as he entered the seating area. The encircling mass of heads appeared to be seething like bubbles on a stew, one from which protruded placards bearing the names of the ingredients.

Most of the flags and banners were Irish. The rest belonged mainly to this morning's disputants: Tricolours borne by the one thousand supporters who had come across the sea from France, Russian flags carried by the fifteen people who had come across town from the Soviet Embassy.

Apple went to his seat. It was on the first line. Rarely had Apple sat at the front in theatres and suchlike. His audience career had been spent in dim back rows, where he wouldn't annoy those behind him or be the butt of sarcastic jokes. This time he wanted to sit at the front. He hoped he wasn't being too obvious.

Settled among the smell of rain-damp clothing, Apple did a scan of the court below. Officials and players were still arriving. Dui was not yet present.

Apple sat as low as he could. Idly, he let his gaze sweep around the spectators. He wondered where the caper-watcher was sitting; and if, like himself, he had needed to pay to get in; and if it was any easier nowadays to get your expenses back from Accounts.

Apple's gaze rested on the press section. He picked out the

hawk-faced American reporter. Scoopsy was doing the same as himself: scanning the audience. Apple managed to squeeze a little lower in his seat.

At last Dui appeared below, through one of the archways. She wore a grey track suit. A towel was looped around her neck, the effect of which had a nice casualness. Apple hummed.

Sidling between various loiterers and bustlers, Dui made her way around to the Soviet bench. It was directly across from Apple. The trainer, head severely back, stood talking to his lead players.

In brushing past one of the officials as she went behind the net-stand, Dui had her towel jostled out of place. She didn't notice the change. The towel dangled from one shoulder. Apple willed it to stay there by clenching his fingers and curling his toes.

The towel fell. Dui still didn't notice. She moved on with a confident expression.

Apple shuffled his annoyance, whined in sympathy, closed his eyes with relief at having been able to resist the urge to stand up and point.

Someone else did that, Apple saw on opening his eyes again. A boy in the stands was gesturing wildly; he couldn't have been more concerned if the fallen item were the Golden Fleece. He was seen by Dui. She got the message and went back. Apple let his belly balloon.

Seconds later, her towel once more in place like a yoke, Dui was at the Soviet bench. She sat without delay. Her eyes went straight to the section of seating where it had been agreed that Apple would be. She picked him out at once. Briefly, their eyes held.

Dui turned to speak to the athlete who was sitting beside her. When she turned away, she reached both hands up to the towel. Slowly, almost seductively, she raised it like an unfurling sail, and then lowered it again to cover her head. Apple performed a yawn.

Following that, he made a point of not looking anywhere near Dui, who would, he knew, be acting similarly. This prevailed as the game started, when Apple began to dwell on the non-caper situation; particularly, on how he could derive some career benefit therefrom.

Nothing occurred to him as the minutes passed—nothing, that is, which could be treated seriously. He decided to leave that quest to simmer at the back of his head, and meanwhile concentrate on benefits of a more earthy, immediate nature: the furtherance of his relationship with Dui.

Apple looked at his watch. He saw that he had time to spare before he was due to make his own signal, which would be for the KGB, just as Dui's had been for the Brits.

Leaving his umbrella on the seat, Apple got up and crouched his way out. He went to the encircling reception area, where he soon found a row of telephones. They were the cowl type. Bending inside one, glad for his claustrophobia but sorry for the small of his back, he used a coin and dialled the number he had memorised the night before.

The male voice that answered was unknown to Apple. He told the stranger, "This is One speaking." It didn't sound as impressive as he had expected.

"What can I do for you, One?"

"Is there anyone there I can talk to?"

"Depends on the strife."

"No strife. I need a car."

The man said a weary-sounding "Rent one."

"I wasn't given a credit card," Apple said. Into the pause that followed, he pursued: "I need a car so's to have somewhere dry to meet the prospect. She doesn't care for standing around in the rain. Neither do I. And we can't risk being seen too often together in public places."

There was another pause before the man spoke. He asked, "When d'you want it?"

"At two o'clock this afternoon would be neat."

"Okay. The car park off Trinity Crescent. Your friendly local contact will pass you the keys at that time."

"Many thanks."

"Drink plenty of orange juice," the man said. "So long."

Apple disconnected. Humming, rubbing his back, he returned to the court and to his seat. He wasn't even slightly embarrassed when he sat on his umbrella.

The game was progressing at a rapid pace. The players ran back and forth with an energy that made Apple's lungs ache. He was glad he wasn't on the court—which reminded him that he had to settle that matter soonest.

There was a foul, latest of many. The crowd rose to its feet with a roar. Among the few who remained sitting were Apple and Dui, who, by arrangement, were using this diversion to communicate.

They lipspoke/lipread. The former they camouflaged for extra safety: Apple, like many of the men present, cupped both hands around his mouth, while Dui, like some of the women, had her hands to her face in the pose of excitement.

Apple: Can you get away after lunch?

Dui: Yes, easily.

Apple: I will have a car by then.

Dui: Smart move.

Apple: How about if we meet outside the Sober Tinker?

Dui: Suits me. What time?

Apple: Three o'clock.

Dui: I'll be there. Let's hang up now.

She dropped her hands, looked away toward the arguing team members and put on a face of outrage. Apple made genuine use of his megaphoned hands by shouting, and since he didn't know what was suitable, he yelled a cricket term.

Finding this vocal act curiously satisfying, Apple thereafter shouted whenever it was appropriate; and, becoming involved, sometimes when it wasn't.

He was disappointed to see play come to a stop for the first break. But then he remembered that this was the moment he had been waiting for.

Apple coughed to himself in readiness. Movements slow, studied, he brought out a handkerchief and opened it fold by fold. He had to fight off an attack of shyness: knowing he was being watched carefully by at least two people, he felt like an amateur in his first play.

Apple screwed his eyes closed. He opened his mouth into a tooth-showing grimace. He started to tilt his head backwards ponderously, the while straightening his spine. Abruptly, reversing the movement, he jerked forward and exploded into the handkerchief. It was a sneeze.

This formed the signal for a negative. Affirmative was a repeat. Devilishly, Apple built up suspense by hesitating overlong before acting sneeze two.

He folded and put away his handkerchief, rose and left. It would have been a good, smooth operation if he hadn't dropped his umbrella.

Apple took a taxi back to the hotel. He was let down to see that whereas earlier there had been two of the anti-British picketers, now there was only one. The woman was powdering her nose, while a policeman was holding her placard.

Apple went inside. He crossed to the reception desk and asked for Whipper.

"Out, sir," the clerk said. He was old and gnome-like. "Be back anytime soon, if God spares the dear man."

"Thank you."

"Meanwhile, I'll be happy to pass on to you a rich joke I got given to me this morning."

Apple heard the joke out. The butt of it was a Kerryman, which butt in Britain would be an Irishman, Apple realised, just as in the United States it might be a Pole and in Canada a Newfie. Apple didn't bother to wonder what they used Upstairs, if, that is, they ever had the need to feel superior.

After serving the clerk a polite smile, Apple left and went into the coffee shop. Watching through the window-wall, he dawdled over tea and a beef sandwich, kept his cigarette-hunger under control, thought about Dui. Periodically he willed Angus Watkin to be kind, supply a car that was roomy enough for two large persons.

Whipper appeared. Apple left the coffee shop, waited, and caught him as he was leaving the desk with his key. Whipper's face gave a twitch of apprehension.

"The sleepstealer," he said.

"That's nothing," Apple said dejectedly. "I'm afraid I have worse news for you, old chap. But it's worse news for me as well."

"What've you pinched?"

"Nothing. It's nothing like that. I can't play basketball. I'm wretched about it, as you may imagine. I might never again get my big chance."

Whipper's face twitched in resignation. "What is it that's wrong with you?"

"I mean to say, never have the opportunity to possibly get my big chance."

"What, Teever, is wrong with you?"

Sadly, sagging, Apple said, "I've been walking so much to tire myself out, so I wouldn't walk in my sleep, that I've brought on my St. Andar's Plod."

"You've brought on . . . ?"

"St. Andar's Plod. It's like St. Vitus's Dance, only calmer. I just can't keep still. I'm continually on the move. I'm just worn out."

Whipper looked up stolidly. He was twitchless. "I have never heard of it."

"Quite common with Sagittarians, I understand," Apple said achingly. "It's a cross we bear. Doctors can do nothing. It's all in the mind."

"Psychological."

"Right."

"Sick."

"Yes."

Whipper told no one in particular, "It's too late to bring over a replacement substitute reserve. The names're in."

"Exhausted," Apple said, giving his eyes a haunted roll. "Every time I do sit down, I doze off. I keep waking up in buses and on benches and so forth. I'd stay in my room, except I soon begin to get stir crazy."

"Oh?" Whipper said. He licked his lips.

"It might wear off in an hour, my St. Andar's Plod, or it might continue. So if I don't show up for practice or games, and I hate like hell to miss either, you'll know that I've fallen asleep somewhere."

"How about if somebody tied you up?"

"I'd go mad."

Still twitchless: "Oh?"

Apple said with a poignant smile, "I know I have all your sympathy and understanding. You don't have to say anything."

"Thanks."

"And please don't worry—I won't do anything rash. I'm not the type."

"Good."

Apple shook his head. "Let's hope for the best, old chap," he said. He patted the other man on the shoulder and moved away in a slump.

That pat, Apple mused, should have been for himself—in congratulation. Anyone else might have been tempted to exaggerate, be wild with his story and heavy with his acting.

Apple went up to his room, which was neat and deserted. He left it again an hour later, after he had spent a quarter of that time in getting the smoke of five cigarettes to pass out of the window. He went downstairs and outside. Rain was still falling steadily.

A taxi had just emptied its passengers: a pair of diminutive Japanese women. Apple circled them widely, rather than pass straight by, as he went to the cab. He got in and had himself taken for a three-minute ride, to Trinity Crescent.

With his umbrella up, Apple stood opposite the gateway of a bottleneck entrance to a car park. He waited. He told himself that umbrellas were very sensible things.

At five minutes before two o'clock, contact-man Malone appeared. He came walking out through the gateway. Apple went directly across.

They met in a sidle, like conspirators. Malone passed the keys over in a way that suggested they were hotter than the car they fitted. He muttered:

"Big red and cream deal at the back, by the exit. Licence number on the key-ring. Parking fee been paid."

Big, Apple thought in salacious gratitude while he was saying, "Thank you."

"Sure and you're welcome," Malone hissed. He peeled off and walked on.

Apple did the same. Passing through the gateway he went along the bottleneck lane. When it opened out into the parking area he kept going, toward the back. He easily picked out ahead a vehicle painted red and cream, but it was a huge trailer-coach.

One minute later, disbelievingly, having seen no other vehicle of anywhere near the pertinent colours, Apple went to the coach. He checked numbers. They matched. The coach it was.

Settling from astonishment, and soothed by the fact of having something to look up at, Apple walked along beside the colourful monster.

A combination of truck front and mobile-home body, it looked to be about thirty feet long. There were cottage-size windows backed with closed venetian blinds. A chromium star was emblazoned on the door, itself located centrally at the side.

Apple used his keys. In order to put down his umbrella without getting wet, he went in the coach backwards. He closed the door and turned. His astonishment came back.

Essentially, the vehicle was a bedroom on wheels. It had a fitted, deep-pile carpet, drapes and easy chairs, all in the same shade of cream, while the bed, at one end, wore a cover of plain red.

Aided by recalling the door's emblem, Apple realised that the coach was one of those luxury items that motion picture companies rent for their stars to use when on location.

Apple went exploringly to a bank of built-in furniture, which included television and a refrigerator. Opening doors, he found

A, a bottle of champagne in a wine-bucket, with refills lying nearby; B, a bunch of black grapes; C, a cooked chicken; and D, a loaded candelabra.

Once Angus Watkin had decided to say yes, Apple allowed, he didn't fool around. It was always a case of nothing but the best would do.

True, it helped Watkin's reputation in the Service, Apple mused. Also, more valuable professionally, it tended to extort results from his people, with the recipient of largesse trying to live up to the implied importance of the deal.

Humming so fervently that his lips tingled, Apple went along a short passage between clothes closets and a bathroom. He came into the driver's cab.

Sitting at the steering-wheel, he spent some time in getting to know all the knobs and switches, lights and dials, of which there were enough to satisfy an astronaut.

Finally, Apple drove off. As he travelled through the city streets, he noted that the coach drew almost as much attention as his own Ethel. He smiled.

The smile held its place, in strong or faint degree, during the time Apple spent driving around outside the city limits. The countryside was beautiful, sparkle-green in the rain, and long before he was due to go to the Sober Tinker, he had found the ideal bucolic spot to park.

"Unless I were bringing in the U.S. President for an interrogation," Dui said, "my control wouldn't give me an old wheelbarrow."

Apple nodded. "Know what you mean."

Dui settled in the passenger seat and closed her door. "You, John, are lucky."

Driving on, Apple said, "Listen. My control wouldn't even

give me the time unless he had high hopes of gaining something."

He glanced down at the lower part of Dui's cape, but, as
before, it was covering the legs, so he couldn't tell if she was in a
dress or jeans. He hoped it wasn't jeans. They could be a problem, jeans.

Dui said, "This contraption is fabulous."

"Wait till you see the interior back there."

Dui nodded formlessly, her eyes roaming the cab's décor and
gadgetry. She dipped a larger, more attentive nod when Apple
asked her if she would like to have a turn at driving.

Switch-over accomplished, and the non-wearing of jeans established, they bowled steadily through Dublin's outer suburbs.
Apple gave directions. He heightened his already elevated spirits by casually playing mentor, as if he had been the driver of
the coach for years.

He and Dui talked easily, topics general. They were backed
by music from the tape-deck and rhythm from the busy window-wipers. When full countryside appeared, Apple had to
stop himself from starting a hum.

Dui asked, "Have you been dwelling on the question of personal benefits, John?"

"Very hard."

"Did you think of anything?"

Apple said, "Well, no, nothing that could possibly help me in
the business."

"I haven't been able to come up with anything either," Dui
said. "I keep thinking along another line."

"Beneficial to you?"

"Yes, though not in my career. But it's a crazy idea. I'd best
forget it. Which way do I go at that crossing?"

They went left along a quiet country lane, where hedgerows

dribbled rainwater. The lane forked into an unpaved byway. The coach began to splash in and out of puddles. Cows in a field of an incredible green stared across offendedly.

The hedgerows came to an end, leaving the byway flat to open commonland, which had a sprinkling of tall, lush trees. Dui, still following instructions, steered off the byway, went carefully over the undulating ground, and at last halted in a tree-ringed clearing.

When the engine had been switched off, Apple said in a tone of importance, "Follow me." He got up and went between the seats into the passage. Dui tailed on behind.

On seeing the interior, she let rip with a yell of delight. Being immediately in front of her, and at nearly the same level, Apple received every decibel of the sudden noise. Shaken, he went to sit in an armchair.

Dui threw off her cape and let it float to the floor. Twirling and prancing, giving junior versions of that yell, she moved around the wheeled boudoir. She looked at and into everything. The skirt of her simple dress waved piquantly high with every twirl.

Recovering, Apple lowered his head in order to get a better view. But then Dui stopped her antics and went back to the furniture's electronics section. After putting music on to play softly, she kicked off her pumps.

"Ah, bare feet on wall-to-wall carpet," Dui breathed. "It feels so wonderful."

"Really?"

"You must try it, John."

"Oh well."

With a swift dart, Dui was kneeling beside Apple's chair. She lifted his left foot. Almost before he had fully realised what was happening, she had pulled off his shoes and socks. Leaping up again, she returned to the bank of furniture.

A tremble of stimulation in Apple's smile kept it on the move. His feet felt bold in their nudity; his hopes were gliding; he was managing to resist the urge to place his shoes neatly together and put a sock in each one—while even enjoying the sly glances down at his footwear where it lay wantonly strewn upon the carpet.

"Isn't this sensational?" Dui laughed. She had brought out the champagne bucket and was hoisting aloft its bottle. "We've got bubbly, no less."

"It's not exactly standard equipment, I can tell you. But let me do the opening honours."

"No, you sit still, John. I once went through a course in bartending."

"I took one too," Apple said. "I scored a four. My Bloody Mary had a greenish tinge."

In about the time it took to unzip a can of beer, it seemed, Dui had the wine uncorked. She poured two glasses, which she brought to the armchair's side table.

She said, "Let's kill these, eh?"

Those killed, the clichés about bubbles dispensed, the glasses recharged, Apple cleared his throat and told Dui that she was wearing a pretty dress.

"Thank you. And it's comfortable. You don't look too comfy in that jacket. Why don't you take it off?"

"Well, I suppose I . . ."

"Here, John, let me help you," Dui said, beginning to do that. Garment removed, she tossed it aside. It floated down to land on top of her cape.

Declining to consider the erotic implication therein, telling himself not to rush matters, for Dui might be offended if he took too much for granted, Apple asked:

"What was that crazy idea you mentioned?"

"Forget it."

"No, really."

Dui said, "I refuse to think about the future right now. This is terrific. Let's drink up."

They drank up. After bringing the bottle and its bucket, and refilling the glasses, Dui went back for grapes. She sat on the arm of Apple's chair and fed him black grapes between serving herself with same. Her fingers touched his mouth.

"Just listen to that rain," Dui said. "Don't you think it's romantic?"

"Yes, it is rather pleasant," Apple said. Knowingly, he refrained from mentioning Ireland's average rainfall figure. There was a time and place for everything.

Dui fed him a grape. "And I love that dreamy violin music, don't you, John?"

Politely, so as not to talk with his mouth full, Apple chewed and swallowed before answering. He said, "Yes."

"I could stay here for ever, just like this, couldn't you?"

"I don't suppose they allow that kind of thing."

Dui leaned in front of Apple to get her glass from the side table. Her face was so close when she paused that he could have kissed her, but he wasn't about to risk spoiling all this by pulling the caveman bit.

After taking a long time about getting her drink, Dui leaned back. She said, "Wouldn't it be exciting if you had put a drug in the wine?"

"What's that?"

She drained her glass. "Wouldn't it be fabulous if it knocked me out and I woke up in another country? A prisoner or something."

"Well, I . . ."

Dui jumped up. "I'll open another bottle of bubbly while you take your tie off. Get loose, John."

Apple said, "I am, I am."

"All this might be old stuff to you, but to me it's glamour with a capital G."

Not knowing whether it was more beneficial to his campaign to admit or deny being accustomed to this sort of luxury, Apple avoided comment by drinking his champagne—after he had loosened the knot of his tie. When he set the empty glass down, his head swirled. He grinned.

After opening another bottle, Dui discovered the candelabra. She said delightedly, "This makes it perfect. Music, wine, fruit, the sound of the elements, and now candles. Style, eh?"

Apple slackened off the knot of his tie another half inch. "Absolutely."

Dui brought the candelabra to the table and lit its seven wicks. She also brought the bottle before settling again on the arm of Apple's chair.

They chatted lazily, drank, ate black grapes. Dui's arm at one stage slid down behind Apple's shoulder, but he knew how easily one could misinterpret these things.

Gulping champagne, Apple told himself he was a shrewd one all right. He was no dummy when it came to the romance department. You couldn't teach a new trick old dogs.

Apple began to hum. He would have continued doing so except that Dui started to stroke his hair, and their rhythms weren't the same. Apple felt pleased that he was the one to make the sacrifice of stopping. It was decent of him.

While her hand stroked languidly on, Dui talked about home,

by which she meant the Moscow flat she shared with her parents, an aunt and two cousins.

Apple considered making some comment relating to the advantages of families staying in touch, but he couldn't seem to get the words together.

And then he became hazy as to what Dui was talking about. This haziness increased with every mouthful of champagne he swallowed. At the same time, he both reminded himself that he had a low tolerance for alcohol and scoffed at such a notion as an absurdity which he had never really believed.

Next Apple knew, Dui was sitting on his knee. Next, kissing was going on, with accompanying pats, strokes and squeezes.

Between kisses, there was apparently some talk about opening another bottle of champagne. Apple felt detached and dreamy, almost like a different person. He sincerely hoped he was having a good time.

"Did you hear me, John?"

The voice was right in Apple's ear, a whisper. He said, "Yes, of course. What did you say?"

"That I thought maybe we'd be a little more comfortable on the bed."

"You did?"

"Yes," Dui whispered. "Come along." She got to her feet and moved away.

In trying to perform the first half of that same operation, Apple swayed far forward in the chair. He kept on going, which wasn't part of his plan, but which wasn't without a certain charm of its own. Gracefully, he arrived on his hands and knees on the carpet.

At a faint squeak of springs, Apple uptilted his head. Dui was spreading herself out voluptuously on the red coverlet. Settling, she did a Mona Lisa at the ceiling.

Smiling also, but with a roué twist to his features, and giving a throaty chuckle, which he somehow felt was expected, Apple began to crawl toward the bed end of the coach. He told himself in confidence that the situation looked fairly promising.

To break the journey, Apple stopped and gave his arms the rest they were craving. His head sank to the carpet's deep, cream pile, which he snuggled with one cheek. He closed his eyes sensuously.

Apple was lulled awake by the patter of rain. He opened his eyes to soft candlelight, rolled over in a movement of comfort, and found that he was lying on the bed. Beside him sat Dui.

She looked around and down, smiling intimately. "You were quite a weight."

"I'll bet. Thanks."

"My pleasure. How d'you feel?"

"Not bad at all," Apple said, in truth. "Booze gets to me fast, but I also make a fast recovery. I hope."

Dui said, "You've been asleep about an hour. I dozed off myself for a while, between doing some heavy thinking."

"That sounds dangerous."

Dui shrugged. "Like a drink?"

"Christ, no," Apple said. "Thanks all the same." He was relieved to discover that he had no embarrassment over having flaked out. Still slightly drunk, he mused, which was quite acceptable: it would make him bolder.

Dui said, "I'll bet you wouldn't say no to cold chicken."

"You're on a winner there."

They had a picnic on the bed, eating with their fingers. For a time, the only sounds they offered were slurpings of satisfaction. It was Dui who spoke first. She did so casually, which gave stronger moment to what she said:

"We probably won't be meeting again."

Apple paused with a wing close to his mouth. He asked, "They're sending you back?"

"Oh no. It looks as if they bought my story about you. That's okay. And actually it'll give me the time I need to prepare, now that I've made up my mind."

"Is this something to do with that crazy idea of yours that you mentioned earlier?"

"Right on, John," Dui said. She looked at him levelly. "I am not going back behind the Curtain."

Apple lowered his chicken's wing. "Let me get this straight," he said. "Are you planning to defect?"

The expression of outrage which Dui snapped into place wasn't totally in fun. "Certainly not, my good man," she said with eyebrows regal. "I'm loyal to my country."

Apple mumbled, "Sorry about that."

Dui winked a forget-it. "But I do want to live in the West. At least for a while. Say a couple of years. Then maybe I could get back somehow, if I still wanted to."

Apple chewed chicken. "How?"

"Perhaps say I'd lost my memory. Something would be sure to occur to me."

"And the KGB would be sure to suspect you of having become a double. You couldn't work in that store any more."

Dui waggled a ravaged drumstick. "Or they would take me on, believing me to be doubling, solely so that they could feed me bum info."

"Or," Apple said, "they'd accept you as straight and send you back to the West, a spook in the field that you'd come to know so well. So the other side suspects you. After that it gets complicated."

"Let's drop it right there," Dui said. "Isn't this chicken divine?"

They ate on until they were picking over the leavings. Apple got up and found paper napkins. He lit a cigarette before getting back on the bed in a cross-legged sit like Dui.

He said, "All right now. To return to this truly crazy daydream of yours."

"It's really not all that crazy, John," Dui said. "And it's certainly no daydream. I'm going to do it. I made up my mind completely."

"And that's that?"

"Yes. I've always wanted to live in the West, which I've visited several times for short periods. Obviously, I score high in security."

"So you have had other chances to run."

"Yes, but the family and Mother Russia kept me in line. Now, however, I see how it can be done."

"That's what I'm waiting to hear about," Apple said. For the time being, romance was forgotten. "I want to know how you plan to stay in the West without defecting."

"I'll simply disappear," Dui said. "Now you see her, now you don't."

"The lady vanishes, or clothes-on-the-beach stuff?"

"Not sure yet. I haven't thought about that part of it, the stage-dressing. I've been too involved in the mechanics after the fact."

"You know," Apple said, "I might be able to help you there. So this needn't be the last time we see each other."

"Help would be great, John, but I'm not going to hang around for long. I might get cold feet. In fact, I'd like to do it today. That's too short a notice. But tomorrow looks like being it."

"Okay, but this disappearance. How can that happen with a lady who's about one foot taller than the average female?"

Dui nodded slowly, thoughtfully. "Long-term I'm not so sure about. The immediate future, that's fine. I have guerrilla training. I can live in the woods."

"Be a bit damp," Apple said.

"It'd only be during the hue and cry. If there is any."

"You mean if you fade without setting a death-scene?"

"Right. My bosses might keep mum. That happens. If it does, if nobody knows I'm missing, it'll be even easier."

Apple leaned away to stub out his cigarette in a built-in ashtray on the bedside table. Upright again, he said, "Yes, it's a crazy idea all right."

"I guess it is," Dui said. "However . . ."

"However what?"

"I think you'd try it if you were me."

Apple grinned. "Very likely."

Thoughtful again, Dui said, "But there's something missing in the mad scheme."

"The kitchen sink?"

"Seriously, John. You know what I should do? I should go out in a blaze of glory. That's what I should do."

"I'm not with you, Dui."

She got off the bed and began to pace in her bare feet. When she started talking, it seemed as though it were as much for herself as for Apple.

"What would be nice for the family," she said, "would be if I left the perfume of good intentions behind me, not the possible smell of desertion. You see how this idea developed from thinking benefits?"

"It would also be nice for you, in the future, if you wanted to go back to the Soviet Union. Met with a bouquet instead of a brick."

"Sure. I wasn't forgetting that. And the best way would be to make it appear as though I'd been about to pull off a real hot spook coup. Then something happened. Somebody, but not me, slipped up. Wouldn't that be lovely?"

"And possible," Apple said, warming to the scheme and ignoring a twinge of envy. "You could spin a tale to your control, ease into something new from the situation you've established with me."

Dui said, "Right. I switch from low gear to high. The tale has to be good."

"I think I know the very one."

"You do?" Dui said. She stopped pacing and held out both hands. "Give."

"You tell your control that you're getting me to defect," Apple said.

"You, John?"

As Dui's hands began to sink, Apple added, "Maybe not. I'm only a substitute reserve basketball player, after all, not a bigwig. I'd make nice press propaganda, but I'd be no sensation."

Dui came to the bed. Smiling tentatively, she said, "The whole British basketball team would. What if I said that I was getting them all to defect?"

"You'd be talking about the hottest coup of the year. When it doesn't come off, your boss just has to be convinced that you've been done in to prevent it happening."

"Yes. The wilder the better."

Apple laughed. "The whole thing is wild."

Dui didn't laugh. She gave a quiet smile. "But I'll do it," she said, nodding firmly. "I usually do what I want, and get what I want."

There was a definite change in the atmosphere, Apple sensed. He said, "Oh?"

Dui kneeled on the bed and in that position moved up until she was beside Apple. With her hands on his shoulders she eased him flat. She leaned down to him and slowly put her lips onto his brow, next his nose, last his mouth.

Apple put one hand on Dui's back, the other on the nape of her neck. He was slow to start returning the kiss, but when he did, it was with an erotic gentleness.

The noise made them snap off the kiss as they both jumped. In fair unison they asked, "What's that?"

The noise coming again, Apple and Dui sat bolt upright. If they weren't players in the spy game, Apple reflected sadly, they wouldn't be responding like this.

He said, "It came from that way."

Dui said, "No, the other way, seemed to me. Let's check." She scrambled off the bed and moved toward the coach's front.

Apple got to his feet right there, by the window which gave out onto the rear. Unconscious of the swift movement, he pushed up the knot of his tie before reaching to the closed venetian blinds.

Carefully he opened two slats. Throughout his following scan, he saw nothing; nothing, that is, apart from pretty countryside. There was no person, animal or object to connect with the noises, which had been a metallic thud-click. It could have been made by a weapon, a camera, or any of a hundred innocuous entities.

From the front, inside the cab and unseen, Dui called out, "It seems clean here."

Just as Apple was about to make the same report, he saw a movement. It came from within a nearby clump of bushes and trees. A figure could be glimpsed through the foliage. The impression was male, and now there came the flash of a man's cap.

Over his shoulder, Apple called tersely, "Start the motor, please. Let's go."

"What's up, John?"

"Someone's here, closing in. And possibly more than one. It might be nothing, but there's no sense in taking chances. Agreed?"

Dui called, "Agreed 100 percent."

"Let's get the circus rolling."

The starter whined, the engine mumbled to life, Dui said, "Here we go." The coach moved forward.

Apple was as unprepared for the lurching as he was for the bodywork's groan and squeak. It felt and sounded like being on a storm-lashed yacht.

Apple was sent reeling backwards, then shoved across to the opposite wall. Bouncing off that, he was flung onto the bed, but had barely settled from his landing before he was tossed off. He thudded to the floor.

As he sat up, he saw that the candelabra had fallen over. Its flames were directly on the table's surface. Apple jumped to his feet, crashed against the furniture, blundered away, forged forward, managed to reach the candles. It took seven panted breaths to blow them out.

Dui shouted, "Are you all right?"

"Perfectly," Apple said as he overbalanced backwards.

"What're you doing?"

He arrived safely in a chair. "I'm just setting things straight."

"Have we a tail?"

"I'll check on that in a moment."

The champagne bucket fell over. Its contents of bottle and melted ice emptied neatly into Apple's lap.

He gasped at the coldness, winced as the bottle thudded onto his thigh, despaired at the cruelty of fate. Briefly it occurred to him that this whole deal was like a form of Angus Watkin torture.

Empty champagne bottles came rolling across the carpet. In getting down to the floor to retrieve them, Apple put his hand on a grape.

Above the bodywork's wailing, the rumble of wheels on ground and the motor's clutch-ridden hum, Dui called, "I'm working it out." She sounded stimulated.

"What? This exit?"

"No, my non-crazy idea. It's getting neat."

Apple wiped squashed grape off his hand. "Good."

"I'll ask my control to organise a light aircraft to whisk the five British players to the nearest Iron Curtain fold. That's easy. And I'll insist that we keep that end of the affair simple in respect of personnel."

"So there'll be more cagey bees at the stadium who could be thought blameworthy when the deal fails?"

"Precisely," Dui shouted. "Then I have to get together the equipment for living rough."

"Maybe you could use this," Apple said loudly. "Steal it, in quotes." He began to crawl in pursuit of stowables.

Dui thought about it. At last she threw back, "It's too noticeable, sad to say. I need a small tent and blankets and stuff. The question is, how do I buy 'em without having it known about?"

Apple, who now had all moveables stowed, called out from his all-fours position, "You don't. I get them for you."

"You do?"

"Yes. Through my control. I tell him the coach was a big fat flop with you. Its luxury you found offensive. You're the camping type."

"That's top good, John. You're a genius, to mention nothing of being an angel."

"My pleasure," Apple said. Sodden of groin, he got up. Fleetingly he remembered a scene of early childhood with himself sitting frozen in class, having been betrayed by his bladder-control. Even fleetinglier, he wondered if that had been his first blush attack.

With lurches and staggers, Apple reached the rear window. He peered between slats. He saw that, although there was no noticeable difference in the coach's racket and jive, it had left the uneven meadows behind and was now on tarmac.

The second-class road wound along between high hedges. There were several vehicles following; they flashed in and out of view through foliage. The first car was being driven by a girl.

Apple shouted a review of the situation to Dui, who answered, "Fine. But listen. Back to my caper. I'm going to arrange it for tomorrow evening. That's when the British team has a game on, isn't it?"

"I think I heard that, yes."

"So lots of bustle and fuss. Confusion helps. And I'll stick to the three real stars, the name players, not the whole team."

"That's a bit less fantastic."

"I'll say they'll be ready to go when they arrive at the stadium tomorrow night. They're nearly always together, those three, so that'll look okay."

"Yes, it's neat," Apple shouted. A truck had cut in behind and was staying close to the coach, thereby hiding from view the following cars.

"It could be better," Dui called. "Neater. If I could get them to seem to be giving a signal, or loitering overlong outside, that would be lovely."

Apple yelled that he might be able to think of something.

After which, a mammoth sway of the coach sent him flying sideways onto the bed. This he managed to turn into an intended-seeming roll, so that he could go on and get smartly to his feet at the other side.

While the act was good for his spirits, it reminded him of his sopping groin, for he had been standing with legs spread.

Dui shouted, "I wish I could think of some way to help you, John. I'll work on it."

Apple suggested that for the moment they think about the tailing situation. His ardour was cold and wet. Because of that and the possible shadow, he had lost interest in the coach. The next stage, as far as he was concerned, was a tent.

Houses began to appear. By the time the truck turned off, the road had become part of a suburb. The traffic coming along behind was dense. Apple gained nothing by scrutinising every vehicle.

Also by that time, Apple and Dui had hoarsely agreed that they ought to separate as soon as they reached town; that they could afford the risk of communicating by telephone; that tents were wonderful.

After a final check on the road behind, Apple set off toward the cab. He went in spurts and untidy swoops. His arms were as busy as a shadow-boxer's.

As had been the case from the moment that the coach had started moving, Apple wore a severe expression. It was there to show himself that the circumstances were dangerous and harrowing, alarming and possibly ruinous; anything, in fact, except farcical.

After bumping through the short passage, Apple reached the cab. He was coldly surprised that he hadn't been thrown into the bathroom and onto the lavatory. With extra care, he sat in the passenger seat.

"There you are," Dui said.

"In person." He was impressed to see that she had possessed the presence of mind to collect her cape and shoes along the way. "What now?"

Following a discussion on the how/where of Dui's departure from the coach, and Apple's assumption of its steering-wheel, as well as some failed speculation on the who/why of the person who had interrupted their country interlude, Dui said:

"I still haven't thought of a way to give your career a shot in the arm, John. It isn't fair. I'm the one who's getting all the help."

"Mmm," Apple mumbled, his eyes on the shapely thighs that protruded from under the rucked-up skirt. He told himself he had a one-track mind, fortunately.

Dui took a hand off the wheel to make a giving gesture. "You're doing so much for me, John."

"And I'm going to do a bit more," Apple said. "I'll get you a car." When Dui's bouncy, leggy response to that had died down, he added, "I'll do more still."

"What else can you do?"

"I'll ask the British stars to help—without giving too much away, of course."

Reaching across to squeeze his knee, Dui said, "John, that's fabulous. But will they cooperate?"

"I'll ask them to do it as a favour to me," Apple said grandly, feeling less wet below. "When they arrive at Harp Hall at seven, they'll be primed."

"Fantastic," Dui said. "Then I'll take off to begin on my disappearing act—with, possibly, a certain tall person not too far away."

"How about in the same car?"

They laughed. Other details they talked over until they were nearing the centre of Dublin, when Dui said abruptly that she had the answer.

Apple asked, "To what?"

"To the problem of a benefit for you, of course."

"How wild is it?"

"It's reasonable," Dui said. "Listen. You tell your chief that you're talking me into defecting."

Apple began, "Yes, but . . ."

"I know—a mere masseuse, like a mere substitute reserve basketball player. But forget cover. You tell your boss that I'm a Sickle. Which is true. And which has a certain value."

"A decided value."

Dui said, "Tomorrow evening at the stadium, I show an observable signal to the effect that I've decided, and I'm ready to go. Later you say that, because of someone's bungling, I was snatched from your tender care by an enemy."

"Who could that be?"

"Anyone you like, including the IRA," Dui said. "Whichever, if and when it comes out that I'm missing, that'll put the stamp of veracity on your story."

Apple nodded in piquant thought. Not only was this a pleasant solution benefit-wise, but it would stop Angus Watkin, in the meantime, from deciding to send in a contact expert, which would put paid to the underling's involvement.

Apple was still praising Dui when she found a place to stop. One minute later, after a brief kiss, Dui had gone and Apple was driving on alone—awkwardly in his bare feet. He at once had a further, interior discomfort:

How was he going to ask the three stars to cooperate, do him a favour, when they quite probably wouldn't lift a finger to save his life?

That, Apple thought heavily, was going to take a bit of working out. If worked out it could be.

On either side of the street, there were trees with branches that spread toward each other. They kept the rain off Apple as he went along, running in the uncovered spaces and holding the collar of his jacket upturned.

Farther back along the same quiet, residential street stood the coach. Its keys, Apple had left in the ignition. There was little chance, he felt, of anybody wanting to steal the flashy monster.

Where the street curved around to join a main road, Apple found a pair of telephone boxes. They were both occupied. He suspected, from the way the occupants held the hand-sets casually while staring out at him with closed mouths and defensive eyes, that they were merely sheltering from the rain.

Treeless, Apple ran on. Purely as a routine gesture, he took one glance behind. He was not being followed, either on foot or by vehicle.

A row of shops appeared. The first, a general store, had outside a symbol-sign indicating that inside was the needed item. Apple bustled in.

The store was deserted except for a pleasant-faced matron, whose features sagged in disappointment when Apple said that he only wanted to use the glass-walled booth in the corner.

Awkwardly, wishing he had gone elsewhere, Apple sidled to the booth and inside. He got rough with the coins while feeding the slot, brutal with the dial.

After several rings at the far end, the same male voice as earlier came on with a wary, unencouraging, "Good afternoon. Yes?"

"This is One again. I'd like to speak to somebody. I hope he's there."

"Depends on the strife."

"You said that before, and I'd still like to speak with somebody," Apple said. He opened the door of the booth slightly, intending to hold it at that point, but then opened up all the way when he heard, "Call back in about ten minutes." He needed change.

On going into the booth again eleven minutes later, Apple had a plastic shopping bag. It contained two bananas, a packet of sweet biscuits, some pipe-cleaners, three tubes of glue and one avocado pear.

Soothed, Apple played it gentle while making his call. When the line came alive it was with the voice of Angus Watkin, who asked lazily:

"May I be of assistance?"

To show how alert and professional he was being, Apple asked, "Is the line clean, sir?"

"It is at this end, Porter. For some strange reason I have no information about yours."

"Clean, sir," Apple said, and added his stinger in throw-away style: "Dui Karpov is a Sickle."

After the expected pause, Angus Watkin, who hated slang, asked, "You mean the young lady is a member of the Komitet Gosudarstvennoi Bezopasnosti?"

"Precisely, sir."

Squashingly: "That, Porter, is not too surprising. Any Soviet group travelling abroad has its generous percentage of KGB operatives."

"I know, sir, but . . ."

"And this, I suppose, means that the possibility of information is a myth."

"Through a cousin, yes," Apple said. "But . . ."

"So," Angus Watkin said, "the young lady seems to have

pulled the wool over your eyes. What purpose did she have for doing so?"

"Simply to establish a relationship by means of a promised prize of info. That done, relationship firm, her true aim came to light. But then, the whole thing was nearly ruined. I managed to save the day, however."

"You obviously want me to ask why the near ruination. Take it as asked, Porter, and stop trying to be clever."

Apple let the booth's door close. All along, he had opened it during bouts of listening, closed it while speaking. He ignored the fact that this activity was being observed avidly by the shopkeeper from around a stack of canned goods.

"It was that vehicle I was supplied with, sir."

Angus Watkin said, "You will, of course, go on from there to explain, exactly, what was amiss with said vehicle."

Knowing that the coach and its victual additions had to have been the work of his control, Apple took pleasure in saying in a voice tinged with astonishment:

"They sent me a super-luxury mobile home. A brothel on wheels. It's quite absurd. Dui Karpov hated it, which is most understandable. She was offended by its ambience, and disgusted with the extravagance."

In a slow, steady voice Angus Watkins said, "And she no doubt talked about the world's millions who were homeless and hungry."

"You are absolutely right, sir," Apple flattered briefly as a form of counterbalance.

"While she was eating black grapes."

"Er . . . yes," Apple said. "I ditched the coach soonest. It's on Conception Avenue."

Drily: "Thank you for letting us know."

"However, I believe I was able to prevent the association

ending in disaster. We'll see. In fact, we'll see tomorrow night, at the basketball stadium, before the knock-out game, when she signals."

Angus Watkin gave one of his sighs. "When she signals about what, Porter? Surely the interlude is over, now that we know what the lady is."

"Oh yes," Apple said. "I forgot to mention that. Silly of me. I dare say I ought to have told you at once that Comrade Karpov, an officer in the KGB, is seriously considering a defection."

The pause this time was longer. It went on so long that Apple himself, growing nervous, was the one to break it. He did so with a businesslike:

"I shall need a tent, blankets, basic foodstuffs, cooking utensils. I also need a car. I intend to woo the lady into doing what I want with a spot of real camping. Though that, of course, might not be necessary. It depends on the signal. We've agreed on two."

"Two, Porter?"

"One to say she's undecided, one to say she's ready to defect immediately."

Angus Watkin, voice lazy again, asked, "And the young lady desires to defect to the Republic of Ireland, Porter?"

"Oh," Apple said after a pause of his own. "No."

"Of course not. She wouldn't be a great deal of use to us over here, would she?"

Humbly: "No, sir." He told himself he should have known better than to put the needle in.

"Therefore, naturally, you will be planning to take Miss Karpov up into Northern Ireland. You will, no doubt, have heard somewhere that that corner section of the island is British, a part of the United Kingdom. You are not, after all, a fool, Porter."

"No, sir," Apple mumbled. "And yes, sir, that's what I'm planning on doing."

Angus Watkin went on smoothly, "Furthermore, being no fool, you will know exactly what to do on crossing the border with your defector, won't you, Porter?"

Taking a chance on bluff, Apple said, "Yes."

"Then, tell me, please. The standard routine seems to have slipped my mind."

Apple looked drearily through the glass wall. He noticed the woman as she dodged out of sight behind canned goods. That this gave him no ideas struck him as wrong, poetically unjust. He sighed.

Angus Watkin, apparently deciding that his point had been made, said, "Ah yes, now I remember. It's simple. You intend to take the young lady into a police station, Porter, do you not, where she will formally request political asylum?"

Risking again, Apple said a weak, "Yes, sir."

"Or, more exactly, you will usher, not take. I imagine you will not wish to involve yourself by also entering the station, will you, Porter?"

Faintly: "No, sir."

"Very well," Angus Watkin said in a different tone. "Now give me the bare details relating to equipment and signals, and then go away."

"Good day," Apple told the woman.

"Good day," she said, not coming out into view. "Thank you."

Disconsolately swinging his plastic bag, Apple left the shop and walked off into the steady rain. He felt damper inside him than on the surface.

But the latter state, presently, became the stronger, the penultimate in wetness, for as he recovered from his verbal defeat, he recalled that he had left his umbrella in the coach. Since it had been a present from a friend, he went back to get it. He got lost.

Apple was so sodden all over by the time he had retrieved the umbrella, that he decided out of perverted spite to leave it down. He strode away from the coach in general discomfort, which he preferred to a discomfort centralised.

Some balm for Apple's spirits came from the satisfaction of seeing only engaged taxicabs; plus indulging in a short, and immediately withdrawn, vilification of the umbrella-gifting friend.

Further balm came when, seeing a ragged girl in a doorway, he was able to unburden himself of the plastic bag in a manner that was morally acceptable. The glue and pipe-cleaners, he had already thrown away.

It had been such a joke-on-you day that, as he was about to enter his hotel, Apple looked around for the vacant taxi which always appeared when you had stopped searching. There were no vacant taxies. Apple was so unamused that it made him laugh.

He stopped on seeing that the placard-bearing anti-British females were no longer across the street. There was only a forlorn-looking policeman.

Apple went inside the hotel, got his key and squelched upstairs. The corridor was dim, the evening lights not yet having been turned on. Apple found his way more by memory than sight.

As he went along the corridor, he was thinking about the long, hot soak he was going to take, the meal he would get sent up to his room, the early night he was going to have. Not until he had stopped by his door did he see the figure.

It appeared as a blur over his right shoulder, a fast-moving blur. He whirled. Releasing the key to his room, he hurled himself into battle.

The figure was male. This Apple could tell by the masculine grunt that erupted when he landed his first blow, a crack on the skull with his umbrella. That the sound held more surprise than pain Apple took as a compliment.

The man fell back. As he did, his right leg came curving up in a kick. It missed, but the attempted action established an important factor: the stranger had been trained in unarmed combat, therefore the odds were greatly in favour of his being in espionage.

The man arrived with his shoulders to the wall of the corridor. Apple, closing in, raised his weapon high for another strike. His wrist was grabbed; and he himself took a similar grip when the man was slow with a judo chop.

This impasse was short-lived. After some seconds, during which the only sounds were of scuffling, heavy breathing and the squeak of wet shoes, Apple broke free and stepped back swiftly.

As though he were holding a rapier, he made a thrust with his umbrella. It was the wrong move. A super-fast kick from the stranger sent the umbrella flying.

From then on, everything was faster. Standing toe to toe, Apple and the man exchanged blows, none of which landed with force. The kicks from either side were deflected.

Pleased with his performance, as well as being stimulated by the unexpected encounter, Apple boldly decided to try a move which he had been taught in theory in Training Three but had never tried.

He sank quickly to his haunches while flinging both arms down, and then, with no pause between, shot upright again with his arms zooming their fists out like catapulted rocks.

It was smooth. But the stranger wasn't there. He had slipped aside. Apple's fists and body met only emptiness. He stumbled forward.

That stumble became a headlong stagger: he had been rugby-thumped in the small of the back. With a wilder version of his arm-waving in the coach, he was able to recapture his balance.

In the hopes of warding off more rugby-thumps, Apple tried to run. It was another mistake.

Apple's legs tangled. He was flung completely around and then thrown backwards. He hit the carpeted floor with a crash that knocked his lungs empty.

He was still squealing them full, and wondering what clever thing to try next, when the stranger came down on top of him. The air left his lungs again.

Apple was too concerned with his breathing to pay much attention to what was happening fight-wise. In any case, as he had already realised, this was no battle to the death; it was a punch-up for reasons unknown.

Almost simultaneously, there were three changes in the situation. The ceiling lights came on, Apple got his breathing under control, and he found that he was helpless in a nerve-binding grip.

The stranger was right above him. Apple stared up into the bland face of a man aged around thirty. He wore an ordinary dull-coloured lounge suit with dandruff on the shoulders. His tie had an Oxbridge stripe.

The accent matched when he spoke, saying with the minimum of gasp, "You are, I believe, agent One."

Apple said, panting where he had intended snarling, "I don't know what you're talking about."

Releasing his grip, the stranger began to rise. He quoted a series of numbers before saying, "Mr. Watkin asked me to drop by." His style was casual-slick, like the cads of yesteryear. "I'm your back-up."

Apple sagged. Tiredly he asked, "So what the biblical-sense did you attack me for?"

"I didn't. You attacked me."

That, annoyingly, was true, Apple had to allow. "Then, why didn't you say something to stop me?"

Upright now and patting his suit neat, the man smirked. He said, "What they don't teach at Damian House, and what I've found out for myself, is that no one listens to anyone in a pitched brawl."

That this was also probably true gave Apple further annoyance. He would have bet, however, that it wasn't why the fight had endured. More likely than not, the operative had been delighted to accept the gratuitous action: in field work, dull times outnumber the exciting twenty to one.

Bending slightly with arm extended, the man asked, "Like a hand up?"

"No, thank you very much," Apple said, cool. He got to his feet. "I hope I didn't hurt you too much with that last uppercut to the ribs."

Curtly, voice gratingly on edge: "What uppercut? I wasn't hit with any uppercut. As a matter of fact, I wasn't hit with anything."

"Of course not," Apple said smoothly. "I'm glad you're only bruised." He leaned on the corridor wall, opposite where the man had taken up a lean. "What do I call you?"

The man shrugged. "Whatever you like. I haven't been given a number-name in this caper. How about calling me Manchester City? It rains there more than it does here."

Apple, nodding, said, "Okay." The nod was also for his having decided that he didn't like the man. It had nothing to do with the fact of Manchester City's being the perfect espionage-agent height of five feet eleven inches, for Apple was no height-ist. All heights were equal, in his view.

What he disliked about the man was that casual-slick atti-tude, as though he had seen it all and never batted an eyelid. Apple suspected himself of being envious.

"This is for you," the man said, swinging his arm up quickly. "Catch."

What Apple caught and put in his pocket was a key-ring. He did so absently while telling himself, to be fair, that he was also being influenced by cynicism in his response to the man. Be-cause a valuable defection had come into the caper, he was suddenly important enough to merit a back-up.

Which, Apple reminded himself, meant that Angus Watkin had completely bought the story.

He asked, "The keys're for the car I ordered?"

"That's right," Manchester City said, looking as if he wanted to yawn. "Around noon tomorrow. Requested equipment inside. Same car park as before, if you remember where it was."

You couldn't blame him, Apple thought in the man's defence. Nobody liked being number-nameless, especially if there was a One in existence. Even so, Apple said:

"I won't ask you in for tea and muffins."

"Thank Christ," Manchester City said, moving away. "Bye."

"See you around."

"No you won't. I'm good at my job."

A moment later, alone, while stooping to retrieve his room-key and umbrella, Apple wondered if Manchester City was go-ing to be a nuisance.

CHAPTER 5

At ten o'clock the following morning, Apple was in the lobby of his hotel. He had a niche to himself right beside the glass doors that led to the dining room. His position allowed him to keep hidden from anyone who might create problems, such as Scoopsy or Whipper, as well as have an eye on those who were still at breakfast.

His own early meal, which had been sent up to his room, Apple had treated like a finicky child. He had been too preoccupied to take advantage of the mountainous Irish break to a night's fast.

He was that way still; still without an answer to the question of what he was going to say to the three British basketball stars once he had got them together—and that part of it might not be so easy.

Apple was pinning his hopes on getting a flash of brilliance, one to hand him a story that would make his request for cooperation not only believable but acceptable.

Now, through the glass doors, Apple saw vertical movement at the large table where sat a dozen members of the entourage. One of the stars was rising.

Tossing down his napkin, the player called Wayne, who was six feet nine inches tall, left the table and came languidly toward the exit. As Apple knew, the team would be spending a restful day because of their game in the evening.

Wayne came out of the dining room. He began to pass the niche, but halted when Apple, leaning forward like a masthead, said, "Good morning."

The athlete stared. "Eh?"

Smilingly: "May I have a word with you?"

Already ending his halt, Wayne said a dead-voiced "Piss off." He walked out of sight.

Charming, Apple thought, his smile greying at the temples. But perhaps understandable in the circumstances. Also, it seemed, very final. Nor was there any reason to hope that the response from the other pair of stars would be any warmer.

In fact, Apple reckoned, it could make the situation worse if he tried any more of this direct-approach stuff. Better to plan differently.

Apple moved on at an amble.

He realised that he would now need a flash of double or even triple brilliance in order to come up with an idea of talking to the stars, and one of quadruple strength to conjure up a story to peddle to them that would need no suggestion of cooperation.

The task loomed as impossible. Apple, ambling around the lobby, shook his head and gave a wry smile.

He wondered if he would be wise to give up on this scheme, plan not at all instead of plan differently. The stage-dressing wasn't all that vital.

A glance outdoors through one of the front windows showed Apple that, although the rain was light, none of the anti-British picketers had returned.

He sighed for defeatism, then straightened his back in the name of implacability. He told himself with features determined that he would have to give it a go.

But how?

Next, Apple's features took on a coziness as he realised that he could try using his favourite food for thought—if it could be found.

He left the hotel.

Ten minutes later, only slightly damp from his hurry through the drizzle, Apple was sitting in a snack bar, on a stool by the counter.

This was his second stop. At the first cafe, he had asked, as he had here before sitting, if the necessary ingredient for his brain-food was available.

Soon the waitress was putting on the counter tea things and a plate of hot toast. The toast was liberally spread with the essential lemon-flavoured marmalade.

Apple began to eat—with an appetite. He was glad he had been shrewd enough to skip breakfast.

Nothing happened on slice one. Apple poured out a cup of tea. After sipping, he began to eat again. Half-way through slice two, a blob of marmalade fell to his plate. He scooped it up, licked it from his finger, ate on.

Apple paused in mid-chew. Face still, eyes roving, he thought of playing the part of a newspaper reporter. In that rôle, voice disguised, he would telephone one of the stars.

And say what?

Apple chewed on, his eyes still roving. He saw the pretty waitress, a poster relating to the basketball event, bottles, advertisements, a nudie calendar, tourists with cameras.

Again Apple stopped chewing. He had thought of what to say on the telephone. He rehearsed:

"Hello, Wayne. This is Mumble, of the *Daily Mumble*. I thought you'd like to know that a local beauty queen plans to meet the British team tonight outside the stadium. She'll be without any clothes on. Completely naked. Nice, eh? I'm letting the rest of the team know, but what you might find interesting is that this lush chick intends to pose for pics with the player who's left when the others've all gone inside."

Not at all atrocious, Apple mused with care. With the exception of one small detail. If there's no beauty queen in the offing, would the players continue to stand there?

Hardly.

Apple began to chew again.

He finished slice two and, after another drink of tea, picked up slice three. Only one single bite did he take before stopping. He scripted:

"I thought you'd be interested in knowing that a local beauty queen is going to be at the stadium tonight when the team arrives. And get this: she'll be totally nude. But she won't show herself till everyone's gone inside except one player. See, she wants to be photographed stark naked with just a single basketball star. More useful for publicity that way."

That, Apple decided, was the answer to the scheme. There would be no need for embellishments. There would also be no need to ask that the information be kept under the recipient's hat: he would no more tell his team-mates than he would shoot into his own basket.

Munching happily on his marmaladed toast, to which he granted full credit for his having cracked the barrier, Apple told himself confidently that all he had to do now was make three telephone calls. He would have everything set up within fifteen minutes.

Two and a half hours later, Apple was finished. There had been about fifty calls in all. He was finger-weary from twirling the dial.

There had been twenty-odd calls to trace one player (in a pub), a dozen or so to find another (at the YWCA), and several to have the last man paged at the hotel (sitting all along in the lobby wearing a cassette head-set).

Between his bouts of calling, from different public boxes to make for more interest and less repetition, Apple had not been idle.

He had gone to the parking area on Trinity Crescent to collect the car; had checked the camping equipment inside; had driven out to a street near the stadium and left the car there; had waited in its dry interior until a vacant cab appeared; had returned to the centre of town.

The stars had reacted to their telephone calls in almost identical ways. Brisk at first, they had slowed to a hum and asked for the whole thing to be repeated. What they didn't ask for was a repeat of the caller's name.

After a sandwich lunch, and before going back to his hotel to nap, Apple made what he hoped would be his last telephone call for at least five years. He did know that it would be the most enjoyable of the day's quota.

He found a public booth on leaving the sandwich bar; they were in the same indoor shopping arcade. He rang the hotel where the Soviet visitors were staying and asked to speak with Miss Karpov.

"Thank God," Dui said, connection made. "I've been pacing the floor."

"Now you can do hand-springs."

"I'm so excited. I hardly slept a wink last night. Is everything okay?"

"Fine and dandy," Apple said. "With you?"

"All running on rails, I think. My control swallowed the story of triple-defection."

"That's good to hear."

"He's all smiles," Dui said. "Well, you know what I mean. Controls don't actually smile."

Apple said, "I wonder if he's made a report back to the onion spires."

"Definitely, with a green-light reception. I know that because arrangements have been made here."

"To whisk the stars away?"

"Yes. They'll take off, in quotes, from a private airfield five miles outside the city limits. I'm supposed to be taking them there from the stadium."

"And they'll look ready for it," Apple said, trying not to sound the show-off. "They've been primed."

"Really?"

"And truly. I've fixed it so that not only will they dawdle outside, but that they'll start to look around in a furtive sort of way."

Dui said, "You're fantastic."

Airily: "It was nothing."

"But how did you do it?"

Apple wasn't aware of firming his jaw while answering, "I put a little pressure in the right place."

"Okay," Dui said. "Now what about your own end of the self-glory deal, John?"

"Likewise a swallowing. If Dui Sickle Karpov arrives at the stadium tonight wearing a woollen hat—hey, I hope you've got one."

"I have two."

"Good," Apple said. "A hat which she soon gives to a fan, it means that she's made up her mind. She's ready to go."

"Wonderful. And with fans always begging personal souvenirs, the hat bit is nice and natural. It's so easy to over-do these things, y'know."

"Right," Apple said. He went on to tell about the car and where it was situated. "I'm supposed to be driving you north, to what is jocularly known hereabouts as Occupied Ireland."

Dui said, "There's no reason why we can't head in that direction, for starters. As long as the accommodation's sound, direction doesn't matter."

"I believe," Apple said, "that the accommodation will not be found wanting."

There was more of the same. It ended before facetiousness could get out of hand by Dui hissing, "Someone's at the door. See you."

The line clicked dead.

After returning the receiver to its cradle with a hummed snatch of tune, Apple turned to the door of the booth, which he had been holding ajar.

He pushed it further open and stepped outside. As he did, a young woman bumped into him. It was a light collision. They both smiled and gave forms of apology. Apple walked on.

Seconds later, with the incident already fading from his mind, Apple heard, "Oh, excuse me." He halted and turned. The woman was coming toward him.

She was pretty, Apple now noted, as well as being younger than he had realised; she looked about twenty. Her cosmetics were expertly enough applied to look absent, but her blond hair was an obvious dye-job. She wore a stylish raincoat.

"Sorry to bother you," she said when she stopped in front of Apple, who sagged. "I wonder if you could give me change for a pound. I have to make a call."

"I'm afraid I can't help," Apple said. "I've just used all my last coins."

"Oh dear. What shall I do?"

"Go in one of these shops, Miss. I imagine they'll give you change."

"Yes, of course," the girl said, smiling up at him. "Why didn't I think of that?"

"Because you're not used to making telephone calls from public boxes," Apple said, feeling clever and knowing that he was impressing the girl. "Good afternoon." He turned away and walked on.

For some reason that he didn't understand, Apple was not surprised when, a moment later, he heard from behind him a cry of distress. He swung around fast.

The blonde was in the act of falling. Mouth open and eyes closed, she fell to the ground, sideways. There was a thud as her head hit the arcade's floor-tiles.

Apple hurried back. He was beaten to the girl by an old man, the only other person around in the post-lunch quiet. Between them they got her raised into a sit. While Apple was holding her there, the old man began to pat around in search of clothing to loosen. He panted happily.

"That, sir, will not be necessary," Apple said, his voice on the rocks.

Almost groaning, the girl said, "No, it bloody won't. Get lost, y'old pig." She looked at Apple. "I fainted."

Whistling between his teeth philosophically, the old man rose and wandered off. His day had been made, Apple thought in forgiveness while examining the fainter's face. He saw a new paleness behind the cosmetics and a dullness of pain in the eyes, and realised that she was genuinely hurt.

Which, in turn, made Apple realise that he was suspicious, and understand why he hadn't been surprised on hearing the girl cry out. Before that, he had subconsciously recalled a bit of spook lore: *if a person asks you for change, beware if he isn't holding the money in his hand.* Ninety-nine out of a hundred people attempt instinctively to project good faith by showing their own end of the requested transaction.

The girl put a hand to the side of her head. She said, quietly, "I've got a rotten headache."

"You gave yourself quite a crack."

"I fainted."

It wasn't so much that the blonde was repeating herself, therefore protesting too much, it was more that Apple was remembering how faints happened. Not only did people normally not cry out, they crumpled, rather than fell.

"You didn't do it terribly well," Apple said.

After shooting him a quick, underbrow glance, the girl asked, "Would you help me up, please?"

Apple did, the while telling himself that he could, of course, be mistaken about all this. The blonde might not be pulling some pity-creating game for money instead of outright begging; she could be truly unwell.

Partially contrite, Apple suggested a cup of strong, sweet tea. The girl acquiesced. He assisted her along to the sandwich bar and onto a stool.

It was no chore for Apple to stand there and let the girl lean against his chest. By the time her tea came, he was even planning on how much alms he would give if he was next retailed a story of penury.

"My name's Fanny, by the way," the girl said, lifting her cup. She was pale and solemn.

"Sam. Hello. Feeling any better?"

"Matter of fact, I feel worse."

Apple said, "You could be concussed."

"I suppose I could," the blonde said. She sipped tea. Unexpectedly, she added, "I can't go through with it."

"I beg your pardon?"

"I think you twigged anyway, didn't you?"

Apple parried with "You know the answer to that."

Nodding, the girl put her cup down. "I'm not surprised. Me, I'm as subtle as scrap iron. And as clumsy. I gave meself a real bash on the nut. Jesus, I feel rotten."

"You ought to be home in bed."

"Yes, luv, but I can't go through with this. Sorry."

Apple didn't know what she was talking about. He said, "Drink your tea."

"Don't want it, thanks," Fanny said. She pushed her cup away, leaned off Apple and looked up at him. "Really thanks. You've been lovely, luv."

"It was my pleasure."

"But listen, Sam. I mean John. See, I know your real name."

Slowly, carefully, Apple said, "Ah." He told himself not to push. She was a talker. She was going to make a present of it.

"But listen, John. There's the little matter of the bread that your friend Barney gave me. The fifty quid."

"Yes, there is that, of course."

"Well, see, I *need* it," Fanny said. "It's not just the rent this week, it's the pawnbroker. I can't live without me ear-rings." She went on in a dozily chatty way to talk about herself. From this harvest of past and present, Apple took the tithe which had reference to himself and milled it clear with casual questions. He reaped the following:

Fanny was a prostitute. She had been approached in a pub by a stranger who called himself Barney. He was English. He wanted to give his friend John a good time, but, in the name of fun, John shouldn't know that Fanny was in the oldest profession; he should think he had picked her up. She was to let him go with her to her flat, and there permit intimacy to take place. That was all Fanny knew about it.

Apple broke into a story of how she had earned her sapphire ear-rings. He asked as though more amused than curious how she had found him.

"Barney brought me along. He pointed you out just as you was leaving this here sandwich bar."

Apple asked for a description by saying, "He wasn't doing his undercover-man act, was he, by wearing a cap or a false moustache or something?"

Fanny was vague. What emerged was a picture of a man about thirty-five or forty with an ordinary face and in a raincoat. "He was a darlin' fella. And generous with his money. But then, I was entitled to a bit extra for having to be an actress as well."

"I couldn't agree more."

"But what about this money of his?" Fanny said. "It'd kill me to give it back, and I'm just not in the mood for trade. But I do deserve something for this bash on me nut. Why don't you come and see me tomorrow?"

"I'm busy," Apple said, patting the blonde's shoulder. "You keep the fifty pounds and I'll fix it with Barney. You earned the money for doing that realistic faint."

"You're lovely, luv."

Within seconds, Apple and the blonde were separating outside. Apple walked along the arcade briskly. He was intrigued with the idea of Barney. He mused:

Barney had been in touch, perhaps by walkie-talkie, with a partner who was observing John Teever in his traipse from one telephone box to another, so that he had known exactly where to go when a prostitute had been lined up. Barney could be of any nationality—Fanny calling him English meant nothing. Barney or partner would have entered the girl's flat after she had arrived with her client, who was undoubtedly being observed right now, with frustration.

Apple went out of the arcade and into the light rain. He began to jog. He felt weightless and free and cheerful.

The hatchers of the Fanny plot, Apple mused, could be either his own team-mates, or KGB, or East Germans (even simply fans of the East German team), or local anti-British types. The plot's aim—that was something else.

Apple knew that he would find out sooner or later, but would give it some cogitation after his nap. As well as being intriguing, it would keep his mind off tents.

There was this drunken woodpecker. It seemed to be coming closer through the forest, pecking from tree to tree. Apple hoped it wouldn't come right inside the tent and have a go at the centre pole.

But next, as the staccato sound continued, Apple began on the reluctant process of leaving the dream behind in favour of reality. The latter on the wax, he realised that his drunken woodpecker was fingers. They were drumming secretively on the door to his room.

Fully awake, Apple sat up on the bed. "Hello?" he said. "Who's there?"

A voice answered. Its tone was a heavy whisper. Its language was Russian. Its subject was the identity of the occupant of room thirty-five.

"I'm John Teever," Apple said.

"Open up quickly. I must speak to you."

"That depends on who you are."

"Yek Milyukov."

Blinking with curiosity, Apple got off the bed and took one stride to the door, which he opened. In hustled the tall Soviet athlete. When Apple had closed the door again, he leaned back on it the way your real pro would.

Yek stood uncertainly by the far wall. He glanced around while stroking a nervous hand over his droopy moustache. The impression he gave was of wishing it was time to go.

"Please have a seat," Apple said, keeping his Russian accent slightly broken.

The athlete shook his head. "I'm not staying long. Thank you. Nice room you've got here."

Had he merely dropped by for a chat?—Apple wondered while hoping that such wasn't the case. Milyukov senior, he recalled, was a highly placed industrial chemist.

"Yes, it's nice and comfortable, this room," Apple said. "As well as safe. It's been checked over, if you know what I mean."

Yek looked thoughtfully at the floor. He seemed to find it interesting. At last he looked up and said, "No, as a matter of fact I don't know what you mean."

"In other words, one can talk freely here."

"Even so."

"Even so what?"

Eyes roving, hand moustache-stroking, the tall Russian said, "When we talked before, you and I, there was some mention of information."

Apple straightened against the door. "That's right. Quite a lot of mention."

"Yes, I seem to remember that."

Casually and pursuingly: "There was also some talk of payment, if I'm not mistaken."

Yek shook his head. "You're not mistaken, John. Payment was certainly talked about."

"Well now," Apple said expansively, smiling like a dentist at a treasurehouse of decay. "That's fine."

The basketball player nodded gravely. "Yes."

"Money is a very useful commodity, y'know. The desire to possess it is nothing to be ashamed of."

"Oh, I know that, John. I agree. There's nothing wrong with money."

"Well, we won't be having any arguments on that score, will we?"

"I don't believe so," Yek Milyukov said. He was still allowing his eyes to wander. The impression now wasn't so much that he was interested in some aspect or another of the room, more as though he didn't want to look at its occupant.

Apple asked, "Your father is well, I trust?"

"Very well, thank you. And yours?"

"Blooming, thanks."

There was a silence. Both men cleared their throats like tight-rope walkers. The Russian, his eyes circling the window, said, "We must talk."

"Of course."

"But not here. And not alone."

"Not alone?"

Yek said, "There's someone I'd like you to meet. If you're interested."

"I am," Apple said, while trying not to show how much he was stimulated. He could smell a real coup developing to re-place the imitation. "Just name the time and place. But we'll need to take precautions."

"I'm with you there," Yek Milyukov said. "This sort of thing isn't a game."

"Right. So where and when?"

"The when is now. At once. I hope that's all right with you."

"But of course," Apple said generously, his smile on full. "My time is your time."

The tall athlete made a move forward, gesturing toward the door. "Then, shall we go?"

"Sure. But where?"

"It's just a few minutes from here. We can walk—if you don't mind."

Apple said he didn't. He said it in various ways as they left the room. He would gladly have said he didn't mind jumping out of windows, if it would have helped.

"This way," Yek said. He turned toward the cul-de-sac end of the corridor. "Service exit. That's how I came in the hotel." He seemed less nervous now and had stopped soothing his moustache.

"How did you know which was my room?"

"I telephoned the reception desk earlier today. I think I've done rather well—at least, for an amateur in this peculiar business of clandestine goings-on."

"But business is business," Apple said with a slight wince at his crassness, "peculiar or otherwise." He told himself that there was no need to keep on selling the idea. Yek Milyukov, obviously, was past that stage. He wouldn't be here if he hadn't decided to try turning some of his father's family confidences into cash.

Apple asked, "Who is this person you want me to meet?" He followed Yek through a fire door and onto stone steps.

Over the clatter of footfalls, the athlete said, "Someone who knows more about these matters than I do. Someone who can talk terms and arrange details."

"That's fine," Apple said, but wondered if it wouldn't be better if he, too, had the company of an adviser. He hadn't the vaguest notion of what kind of sums to offer. But, for the moment, he would play along, stall, wait until he had checked with

Angus Watkin—at the same time, of course, keeping himself firmly in the rôle of middleman.

They came out of the building into an alley. The sky was glum, but no rain was falling. The alley led them to a street, where they crossed to the other side. They walked along beside stores, drawing only mild attention: locals were becoming blasé about the visiting giants.

Apple and Yek turned a corner, then another, then a third. Each street was a shade quieter than the last in respect of both traffic and pedestrians. In Dublin, the suburbs start almost before the downtown area has stopped trying to look like a city.

Apple hummed to himself. He was intrigued and expectant. Furthermore, he was thoroughly enjoying a situation which he had experienced rarely in his life—a public outing with a person the same height as himself. He felt only half as noticeable as normal.

After they had rounded yet another corner, Yek Milyukov said, "There it is."

It, Apple saw when his companion had halted, was a large American car. The late-model Buick, metallic blue, stood parked neatly in the kerb. It was empty.

Opening the rear door, Yek said, "We'll wait inside. My friend's due any second. After you, John."

"No no," Apple said. "After you, Yek."

Shrugging, the Soviet player sank his trunk perpendicular. He went inside the car. Apple followed in the same manner. He closed the door and sat down. Like Yek, he sat out of habit with his head tilted a little forward, even though if upright it wouldn't have reached the roof.

The Russian said, after scraping his throat, "Your father designs aircraft, eh?"

"Er—yes, that's right."

"Well," Yek asked, "what kind of information is it that you want to sell?"

Apple had given no answer—had, indeed, only just digested the question's implications—when the rear door on Yek's side of the car was opened.

The man standing there, seen only as high as his chest, said in Russian, "Good-bye, comrade."

Expressionless, Yek began to slide out of the car. While he was doing so, reversing, he declined to let his eyes meet Apple's. He was outside and straightening as the driver's door swung open.

Apple recognised her immediately, the woman who slipped in behind the steering-wheel. She was the Sickle he had seen with the Soviet sports contingent. She wore a black beret and a grey raincoat buttoned to the neck—an overall blandness to match her forgettable face.

This appearance of a KGB agent curtailed the idea which had occurred to Apple: that the original rumour was true after all and he would be meeting the informant in question.

But although Apple knew what this wasn't, he didn't know what it was; not, that is, beyond the fact that in all probability it held no mortal danger for him. It could even be beneficial.

Yek Milyukov had disappeared from the scene. The man slammed the door. He went around the car and came into clear view while getting into the front passenger seat.

Not surprisingly, he was the Hammer who had been with the Sickle at Harp Hall that same time. Plainly dressed, aged in the twenty-five to thirty range, he had the features of a man who stopped thinking about playing poker only when he was playing it.

The motor vroomed to life. Apple sent his eyes to the rear-view mirror, having felt observed. The Sickle snapped her gaze from the mirror and took the car forward.

"Good afternoon, folks," Apple said, speaking Russian with an accent. "Nice day."

Not only did neither of the pair in front answer, they gave no acknowledgement of having heard. They simply continued with what they were doing—the woman driving like a robot, the man splitting his pair of openers. Nor was there any change when Apple asked if they wanted to practice their English.

He concluded that the situation could not, after all, be of a beneficial nature. On the other side of the coin, danger still seemed unlikely.

"If I had a cup, a stepladder and a piece of string eleven inches long," Apple said, "I could show you this real neat trick I know."

There was no response from the Hammer and Sickle.

Casually, Apple put a hand on the door-handle. There was no give when he tried it. He thought that obviously it had a child-proof locking device that was operated from the dashboard.

He asked in a cheery voice, "Any point in me asking where we're going, folks?"

No response.

"I get it, folks. We're on one of those mystery tours. So charming. Please don't tell me any more."

Silence from the front. The woman made a smooth turn onto a broad avenue, the Hammer drew four aces.

Apple: "Jokes? Anyone for jokes? See, there was this Kerryman who stayed up all night wondering where the day had gone. Finally, it dawned on him."

Silence.

"Did you know, folks, that there's no word in the Eskimo languages for *war?*"

Still silence. Apple gave a mental shrug. He was not at all dismayed. The situation, he found interesting. He admired the way he had been brought to the confines of a car, rather than to some spot outdoors; respected the neatness of the woman doing the driving so that her male colleague would be free to deal with whatever might transpire with their passenger. Or prisoner.

Settling back, Apple thought about it.

Yek Milyukov, who seemed a decent type, must have mentioned to someone that he'd had a curious conversation with a member of the British entourage called John Teever. This item would have reached KGB ears, but not given much importance even if said Teever should be an agent of British Intelligence: such approaches were standard procedure in the espionage world.

The quiet in the car was abruptly shattered by a cry. It had come from the Sickle, Apple realised, the hair crawling on the nape of his neck. He next realised that the sound had been a sneeze.

Unruffling, Apple felt too foolish to allow himself to think well of the woman for this touch of the human. He improved his stability when, in stroking the back of his head, he caused the pair in front to tense.

All relaxed. The Sickle produced a handkerchief to dab at her nose, the man sat more in profile while trying to fill a flush, and Apple said, "Marx bless you."

He went back to his muse.

The possibility of John Teever being a spook would, perhaps, have languished when Dui reported that there might be useful information in the offing via the substitute replacement. Then Teever was pushed mentally aside due to the emergence of a tasty coup—nothing less than the defection to the Soviet Union of three British athletes who were in the star category.

But then, excitement over, Dui's control would have acted quickly, as did agent One's, to apply the rules of security to the coup. John Teever, possible Brit operative, was suddenly important. What if he got wind of what the stars planned?

The Hammer sneezed. Compared to the shrill explosion which his companion had produced, it was a mere grunt, and at that much of it was caught in a handkerchief. He went back to risking millions by raising on a bum hand.

Apple was undisturbed by the noise. He had no need to attack with a witticism. His thoughts ran on:

So they go to Yek. He has a legitimate approach to John Teever and is an obvious straight, whereas Teever might have become wary of agent Karpov (who, Apple interjected in passing, probably knew nothing of all this). They use Yek as a lure, handing him the info/father line. He is in no position to decline to cooperate. He succeeds, though ashamed of John Teever for his treacherous intentions, as well as of himself for playing the Judas.

Apple felt a momentary dizziness. He told himself he must be thinking too complicatedly. Nevertheless he went on to work out that the only intelligent course for the KGB would be for them to render John Teever ineffectual. They had to make sure that he in no way interfered with the planned defection of the basketball stars.

And now the Fanny plot became clear, Apple saw. It had been the first try at getting John Teever alone somewhere without resorting to violence. That failing, the Yek plot had been put into motion.

So far so neat, Apple allowed. The snatching pair had used no force, had made no comment, had presented no façade of threat. Should Teever complain to the police (on the chance of his being non-spook) the pair would explain that from his bad Russian they had thought he wanted a lift. Yek Milyukov, of course, had not left his bed all day.

Shaking his head to clear it of another bout of dizziness, Apple wondered what they planned now, those two who sat there with handkerchiefs to their faces. Did they think they could drive around until the coup had been brought off?

Apple looked at his watch. It showed just after five o'clock. Two hours to go.

He wouldn't have minded a nice long sight-seeing drive, Apple mused, except that he had to be at Harp Hall in order to be seen by his own side receiving Dui's hat signal.

The Buick was taken smoothly around a corner. Both it and the broad avenue they came onto seemed familiar to Apple, as though he had seen them mere minutes before.

He asked himself if the Sickle and Hammer were following a plan, staying in one quiet area, circling, in case he got out of hand and had to be dealt with.

The answer being maybe, Apple decided that it was time he did something concrete about the situation. As he nodded at the sensibleness of that, his head wobbled. Real effort was needed to get it upright again.

He had been doing far too much speculating, Apple mused. The cure for which, in addition to cessation of same, was to sit blank-minded for a while with the eyes closed.

After a final look at the pair in front, who were still discouraging sneezes with handkerchiefs, Apple lowered his eyelids. He sighed. He slid down so that his head was resting on the seat back. He sighed deeper. He listened comfortably to the gentle murmuring of the motor.

Apple awoke in a box.

He lay still. He blinked slowly and solemnly like an obtuse owl during the time it took him to sense out the situation. He began with his physical state, moved to the box in which he was sprawled full length on his back, ended with the world that he could see through the two-inch gaps between slats.

Apple's health was fine, he was not too surprised to find. He had no wounds, he had no pains, there was no headache; nor was he tied in any way.

The box, like a tall coffin, was made of cheap wood and had probably been used to transport a piece of machinery; it didn't look as though it would delay anyone for long.

The world outside, soft in twilight, was flatness and a wall and a spread of sky; the impression was of being on top of a flat-roofed house.

Situation sounded out, Apple ended his torpidity. He snapped a look at his watch, raising both head and arm. They sank again slowly when he saw that it was too late.

Zero hour had already come and gone. It was a quarter past seven.

Drably, Apple acknowledged that he had no one to blame but himself for this debacle. He ought to have realised that the Hammer and Sickle were up to something crafty, first from their passive behaviour, then from the fact that they continually had their faces in handkerchiefs—following those phony sneezes.

Apple had to admit that the routine had been well done, and not only in self-defence. It was a pro job. The gas that had been released in the car had likewise been smooth: without odour, with no sting on the eyes, with no after-effects.

Also, Apple thought on, there would have been no problems about transferring the unconscious prisoner from car to building, even if it happened in the middle of a city. With a person in such a state, you didn't bother to try and hide the act; rather, you complained loudly about having to help this drunk. Far from stopping to stare suspiciously, people hurried on for fear of getting involved.

Apple belched—a sigh in dismal drag. He began to dwell on what he had missed, starting with his own bit of career, for Dui might not have made the hat signal if she didn't happen to see him there.

This dwelling of Apple's faltered as he became aware of the lightness of the sky, left completely when he realised what the dusk signified. He stiffened.

He asked: If it was after seven o'clock, why wasn't the sky fully dark?

The answer, of course, lay with his watch, Apple understood. It was wrong—through no fault of its own. The Hammer and Sickle, crafting on, had put it forward to make him believe what he had, in fact, believed.

Zero hour was yet to come.

Apple enjoyed a moment of relaxed cheeriness before going to work. He brought his knees to his chest. Feet horizontal, he straightened his legs with a powerful double-kick.

What suffered most was Apple. The box lid staying solid, he felt as though he had jumped out of a bedroom window. There was neither cheer nor relaxation in the period he now had to spend quietly, waiting for his legs to recover.

Apple carefully examined the lid. It, he saw, was held centrally at one side by a hasp; this he knew by the three bent-over nails in that spot. All he needed to do, therefore, was straighten the nails and force them through.

Apple set to work. He used his pen to gouge wood away from the points of the nails, a coin to prise those points downward.

The whole job took ten minutes, and might have taken less if he hadn't been flustered through worrying about how long the job was taking.

Apple doubled his right leg to his chest. After shuffling to get the position right, and aiming to strike with the heel of his shoe, he lashed up a kick at the three nails.

When his leg rebounded from the blow, Apple saw that he had left his shoe behind. It was speared on the nails.

Apple started to blush. But he had no time for that, no time to call on his latest short-term cure. The sky was growing darker by the second.

Redly, Apple wrenched his shoe free. Using the heel's side, he began pushing the nails through one at a time. He was pinking off into whiteness when he had the points level with the wood. Shoe on, he sent up another double-kick.

There were two crashing sounds: one when his feet slammed against the lid, one when that flap of wood, after flying open and over, smashed down against the box's side.

Stiffly, Apple got up. He stepped out of the box onto an area that was surrounded by a metre-tall parapet. Lying around were empty paint cans and other flotsam. In the centre was a butte of construction: door and chimneys.

Striding to the door, Apple tried the handle. Locked, as more or less expected. And tests showed that the locking method was the unpickable: a bar.

Apple hurried to the parapet and looked over. He saw that he was on the top of a small block of flats. It was five or six stories tall, and new. Across the roadway were other buildings of identical design and the same newness.

Straightening, Apple looked all around in the gathering twilight. The same buildings were everywhere. He realised that he was in a housing development. The apartment blocks were all in the final stages of preparation, being painted or plastered. There were no occupants, no lit windows, no lighting in the streets.

If he shouted, Apple thought, no one would hear but himself.

He awarded the Hammer and Sickle another couple of points as he started to circle the parapet, looking over. That tour finished, he had seen two possible escape routes, but without fancying either.

There was a drain-pipe. It went straight down to the ground. Not for immediate elevation to Upstairs, as Angus Watkin's superior, would Apple have risked his weight on the frail-looking tube of tin.

The second possible escape route was a layer of balconies. Apple went back to that side after another, fruitless tour. He thought about it.

While doing so, he lifted one leg over the parapet, which, being tall, he was able to do without causing himself a discomfort. He rested his foot on the six-inch-wide ledge that projected from the parapet's base. He leaned outward to have a good look below.

The first balcony wasn't too far down. Its fronting rail lay exactly under the ledge. Its white-daubed window was closed, but its door was open.

Apple measured carefully with his eye. A full minute passed before he concluded that the distance from ledge to balcony rail was eight feet eight inches, give or take no more than one inch. After a lifetime of being acutely aware of heights, Apple had confidence in his reckoning.

And he knew to the fraction that when he stood on his toes and stretched his arms high, he measured nine feet precisely from floor to fingertips.

So that gave him three to five inches leeway, Apple thought, if he hung by his hands from the ledge; ample to get the balls of his feet on the balcony rail.

But Apple didn't know if he had enough nerve. He could hardly look at the fifty-foot drop, let alone consider braving it. And if he did have guts enough, he mused, would the gain be worth the risk?

The gain, Apple realised, would now be more than the planned, for Dui. If John Teever showed up at the stadium after this, his defusing, he, being suspect, would automatically be blamed for the stars' failure to defect. Dui Karpov would lose no glory.

Dui's only loss, if he didn't show up, was the use of car and camping gear. She would take off empty-handed in her run for freedom. She would sleep out alone, cold, instead of with company in a cozy tent.

Apple stepped over the parapet.

With both feet on the narrow ledge, he started to lower himself. He didn't look down. Carefully he sent one leg and then the other into the emptiness below; carefully he moved from his grip on the parapet to having his forearms on the ledge; double carefully, he started to let himself down from there.

He wasn't happy, he wished he had never started, and he hoped he could continue ignoring the tiny voice that kept on telling him to look down, but Apple eventually arrived at his full hang.

His senses had been so concentrated on his hands, which were gripping the ledge, only now did he realise that there was something amiss with his feet. They were dangling in space.

The balcony rail was not there.

Even while Apple was gagging on fear, he was seeing the mistake he had made. From that nine feet stretched-out height of his, he had forgotten to deduct the three or four inches that would be taken up by the grip—by having his fingers bent over onto the ledge.

Apple ordered himself to calm down, to stop searching around in air with his toes, and get ready to risk it. The rail couldn't be more than a couple of inches away. All he had to do was drop that far, hit the rail with his feet and then jump down onto the balcony.

Sure, Apple thought, that's all. And what if his feet missed? And what if they didn't miss, but slipped? And what if they didn't miss and didn't slip, but he overbalanced backwards? And what if they didn't miss and didn't slip and he didn't overbalance backwards, but the rail gave way?

Apple's hands were beginning to hurt. Also his shoulders. He knew, of course, that he couldn't stay on there indefinitely, just as he knew that it would be impossible to get back up again. Yet he continued to hang dead-weight from his aching fingers.

Taking a deep breath, Apple gave the order to let go, now, before he grew so tired that he lost his agility. But he held on. It had occurred to him, at the penultimate moment, that he could increase his height.

This, he reckoned, would happen if he let go with one hand; release his left and hang from the right. It would allow his left side to droop, so that the foot would be lower by several inches.

With caution, Apple began to shift body weight onto his right hand, at the same time easing up the fingers of his left. He stopped. He rebalanced his weight and clamped his fingers back onto the ledge.

It was too late. The top level of Apple's arm strength had gone, and with it the confidence in his idea.

Suddenly, with no formal declaration of intent, Apple let go with both hands. He dropped. His whole system clamoured with nervous shock as his feet slammed onto the rail. It was like stepping down a kerb that wasn't there.

Next, Apple was falling again. He fell inwards. He landed on his hands and knees on the balcony. He was safe.

By the time he got up, thirty seconds later, Apple had recovered so well that he was able to feel foolish for his automatic act of bringing out a handkerchief to wipe his hands clean. He thrust it back in his pocket, brutally, while stepping to the door.

Inside the apartment, it seemed pitch black. After a pause, however, Apple's eyes adjusted themselves. The blackness became a heavy gloom. He had to pick his way with care through the empty, paint-smelling flat to its entrance door, which was also standing open.

The corridor, being away from windows, was darker. Apple took still more care as he went along it and began to go down the stairs.

Guided more by touch than sight, Apple descended in a crouch. This enabled him to take furtive, accidental-seeming swipes at the dust on his knees.

He went slowly down stairway after stairway. At last he reached the ground floor, where he went toward the oblong of greyness that meant the exit. He got there and went through.

It was because he had been going at a cautious pace, thus making for silence, that he took the man by surprise. Outside, Apple was half-way toward the dim male shape before it heard the approach and swung around.

Apple leapt the last yard and, with no hesitation, threw a right-hand punch. It landed unexpectedly on the place at which it had been aimed: the point of the jaw.

Almost yelping at the resulting pain that seared his knuckles,

Apple recovered his balance. He saw the man going back in a stagger; fall to the ground; lie still.

Apple ran toward the roadway. Halting abruptly, he turned and ran back to the man. He stooped over him, lifted his right arm and looked closely in the thickening dusk at his wristwatch. It was the digital type.

Fuming, fumbling, Apple found and pressed the button which activated the watch's light. The numbers said he had twenty-two minutes left before zero hour.

After sparing the seconds it took to put his own watch right, Apple glanced once at the unconscious man's face and turned away.

This time he got further before stopping. He swung around and raced back.

Crouching over the supine man, Apple patted his face and asked in an urgent tone, "Manchester City? Are you all right? Can you hear me?"

The back-up agent groaned. Which, Apple told himself impatiently, meant that he was perfectly fine and could therefore be left to fend for himself.

Apple rose and swung away into a run. He stopped. What took him hurrying back this time was, he insisted, nothing to do with benevolence, but the realisation that Manchester City must surely have a car somewhere nearby.

This proved correct when, after half a minute of slaps, shakes and yells, the agent returned to consciousness and allowed himself to be pulled up into a sit.

"Christ," he said thickly, "stop bloody shouting. Yes, I have a car."

"Great. Let's go."

"What happened? Who was that guy?"

"Ah," Apple said. "Yes."

"What?"

"A Hammer. I was able to get rid of him before he had time to jump on your head."

Hauling himself upright with Apple's help, Manchester City said, "Thanks, One."

"It's okay, but you're supposed to be the back-up, not the other way around."

"I know, I know."

With more sympathy, Apple asked, "How you feeling?"

"All right, I think."

"Then, let's go. Sharp. I must get to the stadium."

They moved off together and Manchester City asked, "Why?"

"You wouldn't be interested," Apple said, which was the official way of stating, under these circumstances, that it was none of the agent's business.

"I know more than you think I do," Manchester City mumbled. He sounded sullen and groggy. "Are you sure it was a Hammer who belted me?"

"Well, it's getting pretty dark. It could've been that Sickle."

Quickly: "Hammer. I remember now."

They stepped onto the road. Apple said, "You followed the Buick here, I take it."

"You wouldn't be interested, One."

"Fine. I know far less than you think I do. For instance, where the hell are we?"

"About two miles from Harp Hall."

Apple asked, "And where's that car of yours?"

It was around behind the building opposite, Manchester City said. He led the way to the unpretentious vehicle. They got in, with the agent, predictably, insisting that he was in perfect condition to drive.

This interrupted Apple's thoughts, which had been focussed with pride on the fact that he had actually knocked a man out with a punch, and which embarrassed him, for he had definitely had an unfair advantage.

As the car moved off, Apple had in mind advantages of a different nature. He mused that he ought to try to profit, through probing, from Manchester City's personality and attitude, coupled with his present grogginess. It would also keep him from worrying about the flying seconds.

Apple realised that he had already laid the groundwork, albeit inadvertently, by saying that he knew nothing. Such statements always left doubts as to veracity, whereas claims to knowledge were frequently dismissed as brag.

And the best way to continue the process of extracting information, Apple knew, was by the reverse of that: giving. You had to disarm.

"Obviously you knew, then," Apple stated, "that I was on a fools-rush."

Manchester City's face, clear in the headlights' backwash, looked faintly smug. "Naturally," he said. "Or at any rate, I suspected it."

"Of course you did. Upstairs must think we're a bunch of idiots. As if I wouldn't guess."

"Right."

Apple got out cigarettes. He lit two, one of which he gave to the driver. Conversationally he asked, "How long did it take you to figure out what Angus Watkin was really up to?"

Sensing the other man's hesitation, he added, "I'll confess quite happily that it didn't come to me straight away."

Manchester City shrugged. "I was told the first part, I guessed the second."

"An easy step, right?"

"Sure. When I heard that in this particular basketball game, tonight's, the British team had to do top well, if not actually win, I knew I was on a chain-gang."

So there it was, Apple thought in satisfaction, with the greatest of ease and after only a couple of minutes of chat. A chain-gang.

His vague suspicion had been right, Apple mused. Of course there had to be a sounder reason for Angus Watkin's presence in Dublin than the rumour caper.

"That's right," Apple said nonchalantly. "But whether this game's the first link or the last, or wherever, I don't have a clue."

"Nor me," Manchester City said. "We'll hear about it all in good time, when it's safe to gossip and blow quiet trumpets. In a week or ten years."

"True," Apple said, thinking of what was more Borges than Ambler, a chain-gang; or as Angus Watkin termed it, a consecutive consequence.

The first link might be the arranged collapse of a man in a Sydney street, the last link, if the chain thrived, would be an espionage coup. For that collapse causes, say, a woman in Paris to miss a plane, which leaves a funeral in the Polish countryside minus a certain mourner, which creates a change of mind in a Swedish industrialist, which makes a young couple in his employment . . .

The most incongruous connexion Apple had ever heard of in a chain-gang was when an East German butcher handed blueprints to a CIA agent in Rome two weeks and eleven links after a teenage girl was apparently raped in Halifax, Nova Scotia. Not surprisingly, more chains broke than held firm throughout, but, being the first love of all controls, they were started time and again.

"So," Apple said, "our Angus sent me in to confuse the issue. He hoped I'd keep the Cagey Bees here busy, occupied, or at least divided in attention, in case they knew about this good-game link."

"That's it."

Apple saw now that even though Angus Watkin was covering the possibility of being wrong—the car, the camping gear, the back-up man—he didn't really believe that Dui Karpov was about to defect. He saw it as a Red ploy to attract more Brit attention away from the basketball game.

"Yes," Apple said, "they could've tried sabotage."

"They haven't," Manchester City said. "And now there's not much chance. The court's under close watch, and the game's as good as over."

Apple looked at his watch. "Not quite," he said, "since it hasn't started yet. But it won't be long now. Do you think you could drive a bit faster?"

At the participants' entrance of Harp Hall, which was at the rear, below ground level, hangers-on and officials were equalled in numbers by basketball players and their colleagues: the evening's rival teams had arrived at roughly the same time. Upward of a hundred people milled around in the stark exterior lighting.

Apple, who had been dropped nearby some minutes before by Manchester City, was watching at a distance, from around the front of a bus. He had seen no signs of his Hammer and Sickle.

People began going inside the large, circular building. Apple smiled as he saw that some of the British contingent were hanging back.

They continued to do so. Others filtered inside, but they, the team's three stars, stayed on, wandering in loose circles, mainly ignoring each other, and making a poor job of acting casualness when they looked around.

Whipper bustled out of the building. He accosted one of the stars, who turned brusquely away, then went to the others. He was either patronised or treated with indifference.

After wagging a finger at Wayne, Whipper went back inside. There was still a small percentage of other players of both teams outside, but not many; it was getting close to game time.

Although reluctant to leave, to stop watching what he, the creator, had arranged, Apple made himself do it. There was another bit of stage-dressing to witness.

Circling the bus and the shrinking crowd, Apple went to the entrance. A guard there passed him through without waiting to see his team-card.

At once, Apple entered the labyrinth. It was made up of the low-ceilinged, concrete, tunnel-like passages which threaded the stadium's below-scenes.

As brisk and full of purpose as the others who were walking there, Apple headed for one of the flights of steps that led to the seating area. He more or less knew the way, having been there at the time of the opening ceremony. Even so, he made two false turns before finding steps. He went up.

The stadium was packed and ready for action. It throbbed with excitement. Piercing the boom of vocal noise were practice runs with whistles, rattles and trumpets.

Apple, to be in a better position, moved around to the next aisle. A girl stopped him. She had an autograph book. So as not to start the near-inevitable rush of similar requests, Apple held up a clawed hand and said he had an attack of writer's cramp, sorry. Blinking, the girl withdrew.

Apple stood in a sag at the aisle's side. He wasn't too conspicuous, he reasoned, for there were many people finding their seats or circulating on private missions. He kept a watch on the seating area opposite, on the other side of the playing court.

Almost at once (she had been waiting for him to show up and roost, Apple knew), there appeared a tall figure wearing a trouser suit and a knitted cap in flaming scarlet.

Apple smiled. He stopped worrying that the girl with the autograph book might be hurt.

Dui came down her aisle. She didn't stop until right at the front railing. After pausing to look all around, she turned back and started up. Only someone with badly damaged vision could have failed to see her.

Three or four of the broad steps Dui took before halting. Beside her stood a woman who was waiting to move into a row of seats. With an impulsiveness that didn't look too sudden, Dui took off her woollen hat and began to fit it onto the head of the woman, who gaped happily.

Transfer complete, recipient's thanks accepted, Dui went on up. Within seconds she had gone from sight.

In order to give observers the impression that he was super cool, Apple stood on for at least three minutes. And his departure had in it a touch of reluctance, as though he were saying to himself that, sure, a KGB defection was all right, but it would be nice if he could watch this imminent game of basketball.

Humming, Apple made his way back toward the labyrinth, from where he would gain the outdoors and go to meet Dui at the rendezvous spot, the car.

At an exit from the seating area, Apple was detained by a pair of gangly youths. They presented their autograph books almost with belligerence.

Hastily, guiltily, with covert glances around to see if the girl hunter was watching, Apple signed the books—and in the first one nearly put his true name.

Both nervous and satisfied, he went down into the bowels of Harp Hall. An atmosphere of urgency seethed in the low concrete passages. People hurried along with grim faces. As he searched for an exit to the outdoors, Apple had several near collisions with hurriers.

At one junction he stopped. He wondered which direction to take, instead of blundering into the handiest.

Suddenly, while still undecided, Apple was grabbed. Someone took him from behind in a full embrace.

As his arms had been at his sides, they were included in the grab. He felt helpless. Obviously, the embracer had been in a stoop, for Apple at once found himself being lifted.

His head hit the ceiling.

His cry of pain came at the same time as a male voice from the area of his spine said, "Got you!"

The captor set off along a passage at a thudding, stumping run. It was unpleasant for Apple. He was jerked about like a cork on boiling water. He felt unable to speak.

His dizziness and nausea from the head blow persisted even though the pain was fading: a repeat seemed likely: the ceiling was dangerously close.

People stood aside staringly to let the pair go by. Apple felt stupid, as well as astonished and sick, scared and void of power. He lolled his head dodgingly, tried to get strength into his dead-feeling arms, wondered what the bloody hell was happening, and poked about in his memory for the remedy to this particular hold.

Curiosity won and gave him voice. He asked jerkily, "What's going on?"

The voice from behind panted strenuously, "Not a thing to worry about."

Apple thought he recognised the accent. He said, "That must be Scoopsy."

"Right on, Mr. Teever."

"Put me down. Stop."

The American reporter gasped, "Can't do that. Sorry."

"Why not?"

"Gotta be sure I get the credit for this."

"What you talking about?" Apple said. "Don't be a lunatic, you lunatic."

"I know what I'm doing."

"I don't. Put me bloody down at once."

They turned a corner. The American said in a voice as jerky as his prisoner's, "Sorry and all that. But I deserve this for the hours I've wasted on you and that Red dolly."

"Following us?" Apple asked. He was starting to recover and managing to keep his head out of danger. "I knew it was you, despite the cap."

"This is gonna be a better story."

"You're crazy."

"We'll see about that."

"If you don't put me down, Scoopsy," Apple said, "you're liable to get two busted knee-caps." He had remembered one of the remedies: a double-kick backwards.

But he knew he wouldn't try it. Damage to recipient apart, the remedy's drawback was that its user often came down flat on his face, the bear-hug having persisted briefly in a reflex action to the pain below.

"I can see it now," Scoopsy gasped.

"What? What's that?"

"Front page. Two-inch banner. How I Saved the Day for England, by Our Own Correspondent."

Apple wriggled. "Stop ranting and put me down."

"We're nearly there," the reporter said. "I'll get a by-line, of course."

"You're out of your mind."

"The Queen might even give me a medal."

His head out of danger of hitting the ceiling now, now that the American was tiring and therefore letting his burden slip, Apple felt better in spirits, but he was still being tossed about like the papoose of a jogging squaw.

"If you don't put me down," he began. He didn't finish, for down he went. Scoopsy dropped him after another corner had been turned. Apple found himself among half a dozen men.

While recovering from being abruptly dropped, helped by many steadying hands, Apple recognised the men as members of the British entourage.

They were all talking at him anxiously as well as calling out through the nearby open door. At the same time, Scoopsy was loudly claiming all credit for having located the lost player.

"I'm not lost," Apple yelled. "What's this all about?"

Everybody began explaining. The confusion was augmented by the appearance, from the doorway, of Whipper. He, too, launched into an explanation after pushing his way to the front.

"So there's no time to lose," Whipper ended. "This way."

"What?" Apple asked dazedly. He was beginning to understand, piece together snippets from this one and that. He did not, however, believe it.

He found that he was being manoeuvred around and toward the doorway, which, he realised, was to a dressing-room. With Whipper staying in front of him while he moved, Apple stooped close and asked:

"Are you trying to tell me that our three star players've disappeared?"

"Yes yes yes. Come on."

"Disappeared where?"

"No idea. Some madness."

"You mean they just walked off?"

"They got in a mini-bus," Whipper snapped. "The how of it doesn't matter. They've gone."

CHAPTER 6

"Gone," Apple repeated dully, shaking his head negatively at what he knew must be true. "No."

"Yes, but never mind that now. My present problem is you."

"Me?"

"You," Whipper said. "We've got to get you ready."

Incredulously, suspecting: "Ready for what?"

"The game, stupid. You're playing."

Apple gasped. He was through the doorway now, and was vaguely aware that the dressing-room held athletes in various stages of undress. The atmosphere was feverish.

"Yes, make no mistake," Whipper said. "You, Teever, are playing in this game."

"But what about my St. Andar's Plod?"

"Forget it, and manage as well as you can. One of the reserves is sick, another just got so excited he twisted his ankle. You are definitely playing. So look alive and get changed."

Apple asked a feeble "Can't you delay the game?"

"Against the rules," Whipper said, twitching. "We either field a team or lose by default."

"Then, find the stars."

"Brilliant. You think we're not trying? Now get changed quick. We've got about five minutes."

Looking all around him while wondering if he could be in the middle of a nightmare, Apple asked, "But why did the stars get in a bus?"

Whipper said impatiently, "All I know is that the driver shouted at 'em that it was an emergency, and they just got in with him."

An official came up with a hold-all, which he thrust into Apple's arms with a gruff "Your things."

"Move it, Teever," Whipper said. He swung Apple around sideways and pushed him in the direction of a bench. "Less than five minutes left."

It was no nightmare, alas, Apple thought. He called to the twitching man, "We'll lose."

"You're telling me," Whipper said in a combination sigh and moan. He strode to the dressing-room door, which, after a meaningful glare around, he closed with a slam. He went to harangue one of the players, who was wrestling with a sweater.

Apple, jittery, sat on the bench and then got up again. He started to undress. His eyes, on semi-automatic, checked the walls for escape routes. It was a comfort to be concerned with something that made sense.

Apple didn't know which he found the most idiotic and disturbing of the two shocks that he was still in the process of absorbing: that he might actually have to go on the basketball court and play, or that he was going to be responsible for the breaking of a link in a chain-gang.

The latter, Apple knew. His atrocious, bumbly playing tonight would soon be forgotten by all except three or four million basketball fans; his destruction of a link, should the truth come out, would never be forgotten by anyone who knew that there was such an entity as Upstairs.

Apple gave a groan, short to match his haste. He knew that not only would he be out of the Service, but that operatives everywhere would toast each other with "Here's Appleton Porter in your eye."

Thinking thus, lightly, enabled Apple's mind to skitter away from another factor. He didn't need to remind himself that when a link broke, people sometimes got hurt. And when that happened, the victims were often listable under Bystander, Innocent.

His scan of the walls had told Apple that, one, there were no windows, and, two, that the fire exit was being guarded by a pair of officials, one of whom had a blandness of form and feature that suggested he could be an agent.

Nor would there be any way out in the washroom, Apple knew. There was no escape route except through that door, and there were too many people around it and beyond it for a full-frontal charge to freedom.

But, Apple mused agitatedly as he ripped off his shirt, freedom he had to gain. He had to get away, because he needed to delay the game while he found the stars, because this game had to be a good one and his own career had to go on and Dui might be able to tell him what had happened, if she had waited around long enough.

Apple, having stripped to his underpants, began to put on the shorts of his playing uniform, in which he had never yet played.

Still semi-oblivious to the bustle and din going on around him, Apple thought about the stars' disappearance—in respect of mechanics, not motive, at which he wasn't even bothering to try a guess.

It was no surprise to him that the players had responded, and well, when told with force that there was an emergency. Ever since the Munich Olympics, knowing that mindless terrorism could happen again, athletes who competed at the international level had been acutely conscious of the danger, and were still, even though others may have become less security-conscious.

The voice of Whipper rose above the crowd: "Three minutes to go, men!"

Apple came alert.

While hustling into his uniform top and then a track suit, he went back to thinking about ways of escape. But he found concentration difficult in the racket that was perceptibly rising in the dressing-room.

Apple had still thought of nothing useful by the time he was trying up one of his boots—the other was being attended to by a kneeling official. They finished together.

Apple next found himself pulled to his feet and bustled toward the door. He was among other playing athletes. They gave off waves of excitation. Apple glanced back at the fire exit. The two men were still there.

Out in the corridor, Apple and the other players were swiftly formed into a single file, with each man sided by an official. More members of the United Kingdom group fore-and-afted the procession.

"Forward march!" Whipper cried absurdly. He was ranging back and forth along the double column like a wagon-train master in the Old West.

The procession moved off.

Apple, positioned about one third of the way back from the front, was beside a fetch-and-carrier. The man appeared to be on the point of leaping upward out of excitement. He jiggled as he walked.

Catching Apple's glance, he said, "This is it, lad."

"Probably."

"Makes you feel like running, doesn't it?"

Which, Apple told himself, was the only answer to the matter of escape. Running. If he got as far as the court, it would almost certainly be too late. He had to make his move somewhere down in these burrows. At the first opportunity, he must make a run for it.

"No, it doesn't make me feel like that," Apple said to the man at his side, who was in middle age but with a youthful manner, like an old Boy Scout. "It makes me want to throw up."

"It's only nerves, lad."

"I know."

The man said, "Don't worry about it."

"I'm not," Apple said. "If it looks like happening, I'll just head for the nearest washroom."

That, he mused, would at least supply some kind of an explanation for his vanishing act. Not that it mattered. Little did, apart from not letting this bunch of non-stars play—though they might have made a reasonable job of it without the handicap of John Teever.

Tense, Apple kept a watch on the way ahead. He soon saw a junction, a branch to the left in the low passage. Annoyingly he was forced to rule the fork out as a possibility: not only was the excited man on that side, but two staff women had paused in the opening to see the column go by.

When it did, they clapped.

"Hope they do that later," the man said, jiggling his optimism. "When we're on our way back."

Apple mumbled, "Mmm." Escape method settled, he was now dwelling on ways to delay the game; or rather, which way to attempt of the several disrupters he remembered being listed in Training Five.

Ahead appeared a four-way junction. It was clear of people. That, Apple decided, was going to be the one. It would serve the purpose nicely.

On looking back to check out the situation, he saw that Whipper was working his way along the column. That fact brought Apple to another decision: rather than risk being detained, he wouldn't wait.

The junction was thirty feet away. Preparatory to swerving out of line for the run ahead, Apple took a deep breath. He coughed it out again nervously as he felt his arm grabbed.

Looking around sharply, Apple saw that his neighbour, the grabber, was gazing up at him with an expression of sympathy. He had given up on his jiggling. He no longer had a youthful appearance.

"Eh?" Apple said. He was aware that the hold on his arm had slackened to frail.

"Listen, lad," the man said.

"Yes? Yes? Yes?"

"I know what it's like. I understand. I, too, got my big chance once upon a time, many years ago. An international game it was, like this. In Toronto."

"Yes? Yes?"

"I was pretty young myself then," the man said. He smiled in forgiveness. "And that night I was a bundle of nerves."

"Yes?" Apple asked, aware that the hold on his arm had now ended.

"Everyone said I was going to be a disaster. I didn't have the experience, see. You understand that."

Apple nodded. He moved his head closer.

The man said, "I didn't want to let the others on the team down. They were all friends of mine. That was much more important to me than—"

"Stand tall, Teever!"

At the shout, Apple jerked around to face the other way. Whipper was there, walking beside him.

"Tall, Teever," he said. "Let's show 'em we're not afraid."

Switching his eyes to the front, Apple saw that it was too late.

The head of the column had already turned at the junction; and now his own section was arriving, with himself blocked in by the two men.

"Let's show 'em what we're made of," Whipper said.

The other man said, "That's the spirit."

The column curved around the corner and Apple found that he was going along, which, he accepted, he had to do short of using physical violence.

They began to climb steps. From immediately above came the roar of a living stadium.

His mind flurrying, his body achingly taut in its lust for fast action, Apple thought of what he could do now. Collapse on the court? Attack a member of the opposing team? Have hysterics? Keep up the good walk?

The column marched upward.

Before he came into the blare and blaze of the stadium, Apple had time only to remind himself in an aside that he could always check the record books for who had won in Toronto.

Whipper fell back. Apple maintained his place as the column, accompanied by the crowd's ovation, marched around behind the nearest basket-stand. Next, it was going along the side of the court toward the British team's benches.

Apple was on the outside, by the strip-wood floor. When the column began to slacken its pace, he didn't do the same. He edged out of line and kept on going.

Almost at once, Apple was leaving the column's leaders behind. He lengthened his stride, though still marching neatly. The nearest exit, in a corner, stood half a court away and was edged with police and officials, staff and strays.

It wasn't until Apple had reached the midway point in his journey to the exit that those he had left behind responded.

Among the voices raised in surprise was one shoved up high in outrage: Whipper's. Then it and the others faded in Apple's ears as distance gave preference to the crowd's roar.

Arriving near the standers, Apple pushed through toward the exit. He ignored questioning stares, especially those that came from the policemen.

Calm down, he was telling himself; hot head never won fair maid nor stoppèd basketball game.

Through the opening, Apple came to stone steps. He took them in leaps. Near the bottom, he stumbled, wobbled, recovered, jumped down to level ground—and entered the labyrinth.

At full speed Apple raced along a tunnelesque passage. His speed was far more for what lay ahead than for what was behind: the others, he knew, would make official arrival on the court their first goal, rather than the apprehension of a deranged substitute reserve.

The passages were almost deserted, with the game upstairs on the point of starting. Apple passed only the occasional staff person as he changed directions in his search for the door, which had to be hereabouts somewhere. It was that one he vaguely recalled having passed more than once.

With his calm shimmying, Apple charged on. There was no hint of pursuit. The only sound came from his basketball boots. They were slapping the concrete like a legion of backhanders.

Apple saw the right door. He could hardly miss it. The colour was bright red. Restrained white lettering said that unauthorised persons were forbidden to enter.

Arriving in a rush, Apple grabbed the handle. He twisted it. Nothing happened. The door was locked.

Apple sagged, beaten. But only for a moment. Swiftly he bent to the keyhole. His spirits reared like stallions when he saw that the lock was of a simple type, one which he could pick without the slightest difficulty.

The stallions put their feet down: Apple had realised that something was missing.

To do the lock-picking job he needed a certain object. He didn't have it. However (stallions three-legged), he recalled that the object, though particular, was more than commonplace.

Apple pushed himself off the door and ran along the passage. His main worry now was not centred on getting hold of the necessary item, but on being able to find his way back quickly enough to the red door.

He skidded around a corner. Braking briefly, he swept by a man who was in the green coverall worn by all Harp Hall staff members. Apple saw more green at the next junction. He turned that way, gasping in relief.

This staff member was female. A scrawny, untidy matron, she was ambling along with bucket and mop as though she had never heard of a game called basketball.

Apple went straight in to the attack.

While doing so, he had to admit that the performance he gave was far from being one of his better efforts.

His overbalancing was badly done, the way he stumbled against the woman lacked conviction, his sortie with one hand into her hair was more scuffle than passing swipe, and his swing around to run back the way he had come made the whole thing ridiculous anyway.

But, having succeeded with his attack, Apple didn't care. And he was relieved, not shocked, on hearing the woman's shrieked anatomical epithet: it somehow balanced the score for loss of dignity.

With the hair-clip clutched tightly in his fist, Apple went

back and made the same two turns. He came to the red door. Kneeling, he probed the clip into the lock.

Seven seconds later, Apple was walking into the room.

Almost everything was red. The main colour challenge came from white—the lettering that Apple began reading even before he started to close the door behind him. He read only those words which appeared over the larger of the hundreds of electrical switches.

AUDITORIUM-ARENA. At last Apple found the one he wanted. He grasped the handle of the gate-switch and eased it down to OFF. Next, standing sideways, he began to push it over. The metal bent without too much pressure. When the switch had reached its crooked limit, Apple tried to lift it back up to ON. It wouldn't go.

That, Apple thought as he turned away, would have to do. Up above, they would first of all check the fixtures and connections there, not think of the power room straight away. The switch, they could fix in minutes, but its sabotage nature might prompt a search of the whole building. Whatever, any delay was better than none.

After leaving the room and closing its red door behind him, Apple took up another sideways stance. He raised his boot and slammed a sole-kick against the door-handle.

And that, he told himself as he flung away and ran on, might do enough damage to the lock to render the door a separate problem. Any delay . . .

It took Apple another minute to find a way out, a narrow flight of steps leading upward out of the labyrinth, during which time he saw nothing of the cleaning woman. As he ascended, he threw the hair-clip away.

Apple came into the reception concourse that surrounded the stadium's core. At the moment of his arrival, it was near deserted, but, before he had taken twenty semi-running strides, people began to come through the double swing-doors that led to the court.

Most were staff and officials. Apple didn't need to hear exactly what they were saying—with boredom or pique—to gather that there was a lighting problem inside.

He went on. He quickened his pace into a full run. Since he didn't know which was the most vital, finding Dui or avoiding his own entourage, he thought of neither. He assured himself that hair-clips were cheap.

"John!"

Apple lurched into a slowing turn in answer to the shout, which had sounded from behind. He saw Dui. She had just come through one of the exterior doors.

Apple was ashamed of the warmth of relief that gushed through him. It meant, he realised, that he had suspected Dui of working some kind of double-cross with the stars.

Meeting in a rush, Apple and Dui started talking at the same time and with the same shortness of breath. They took turns. Dui said she had been running all over the place, looking for him: "The British stars're gone."

"I know. That's why I just screwed up the court lights. I have to delay this game. I can't explain why."

"I wouldn't be interested."

"Thanks," Apple said. "Who took the stars?"

"A zealous and jealous Hammer. It was nothing to do with me. He's nuts. Except for a couple of dozen words, he doesn't even speak English."

"Where's he taken them?" Apple asked, thinking that the man could only be a faceless one; no pro would ever try anything so outrageous.

To the private airfield, Dui reported urgently. West Town

Flying Club. Only a few miles further along on this same highway.

Apple shook his head. "Then, it's got to be too late."

"No, John. There's heavy traffic, to begin with. Also, will he get the prize to board the plane? And if he does, he'll wait till the last moment for me, expecting me to show up."

"Which you can't do," Apple said. He started to move away. "But I can."

"You have a car," Dui pointed out as she fell into step at his side. "It's not that far away."

"Too far. I'll have to pinch one."

"I'll help. I know the job."

Ahead, through swing doors, came two of the British entourage, one of whom had walked beside Apple in the procession. They saw him and jerked to a halt.

"Christ," he said. "This way."

With Dui close behind, Apple went quickly to and through one of the exterior doors and around toward Harp Hall's front. He took a look back. The men were following, though at a less hectic pace.

Dui, who had looked back also, asked, "Should I run a bit of interference?"

"If they get too cheeky, yes."

"Bones or muscles?"

"Nothing too awful. They're innocent. I mean innocuous."

Dui said, "Look over there, John. Taxicabs. Be faster than stealing."

"Right," Apple said. He changed direction. "If I can bribe the driver to break speed laws."

They were crossing the forecourt now, among a scattering of people and vehicles of all kinds. Forms and lights were doubled in the tarmac, its surface wet from the gentle drizzle.

Abruptly, Apple changed direction again. "Come on," he said in a curt tone. "There's a neat set-up. See it?"

"Yes. Yes indeed. What's that expression about candy and babies?"

"That depends on how good a fainter you are."

The ambulance was new, long, sleek and white, with on its roof an array of lights extensive and imaginative enough to please the most demanding schoolboy. The para-medic driver, standing in a lean against the door, was as hefty as a handler of bodies needed to be.

There was no one else around.

To end their strategy exchange, just before they came within the driver's earshot, Dui said, "This is going to turn into a wrestling match if the keys aren't in."

"They have to be by law," Apple lied. He was lying not so much to give Dui confidence but to encourage fate to have done the right thing.

"See you."

"Yes, you will."

They branched away from each other. Apple went left, so as to come up by the rear of the ambulance. Dui aimed to pass near its side.

Noting the glisten of water on the driver's cap, Apple hoped it was true what they said about people who didn't come in out of the rain, for he had the suspicion that Dui lacked talent as an actress.

He was right. Where Fanny had done a refined Barbra Streisand, Dui did a drastic Theda Bara.

When she reached a point some six feet from where the man in hospital whites leaned, Dui stopped as suddenly as if she had come to the end of a tether. The man, seeing this, twitched as though he, too, were on a string.

Moaning, a limp hand raised to her forehead, Dui started on an elaborate sag. The para-medic's response was immediate. He leapt forward and grabbed the apparent faint victim before she hit the ground.

Timing was good. Apple hadn't even slowed. He reached the driver's door and yanked it open and slipped inside behind the steering-wheel. It wasn't until he slammed the door closed that he was seen. The driver looked around. He opened his mouth to shout.

But, as Dui fell onto her back, pulling the para-medic down on top of her, the only sounds were the ones she made herself —moans and whimpers. And it looked accidental, the position of her right hand under the driver's jaw.

Apple glanced down. The keys were in the ignition. Thanking fate, he switched on. Several fumbling seconds passed before he could find and press the starter. When the motor roared to life, he looked out.

Dui, though still holding, no longer moaned. The driver, though still making mute shapes with his mouth, no longer looked put out by the fact of being on top of Dui.

As he let up the clutch and moved off, Apple glimpsed a movement from behind. He glanced back. Approaching at a trot, faces incredulous, were the two members of the British group.

Apple's sole thought in connexion with this, while he put lights on and rapidly increased speed, was that if it came to a male-against-female showdown, in serious, heaven help the three men.

He was heading for the broad exit to the highway, where

several policemen stood lazily watching the traffic, which passed at a lumber.

Again Apple looked down at the array of dashboard knobs and switches. He found the one he wanted by its red light. As soon as he had pressed it, he immediately, instinctively ducked. The resulting siren's shrill yip-yip sounded like rockets whizzing over right above his head.

The policemen at the highway whirled on hearing the siren. Moving quickly, they began to stop traffic.

Apple looked in his rear-view mirror. He was pleased but not surprised to see the back of Dui as she strode away and, closer, the three men lying in a pile.

Traffic being held by policemen, Apple needed to slow only minimally when he reached the highway. He swung into the middle to straddle the white line. There, after bringing window-wipers into play, he put on more speed.

Cars ahead on both sides moved out of the way. The faces of their passengers flicked from sick to normal in the whirling flash of the yellow light on the ambulance roof. The siren yipped on. It drowned out everything except the radio of a passing car.

Which gave Apple an idea. Once again, he checked the range of instruments. The radio was easy to find. What took longer was getting it off hospital-call. The rest was a matter of twisting the knob to find the right tone of voice.

". . . *been told that it's nothing to worry about,*" the commentator was saying. "*A fuse or something. So that's good news. In any case, the crowd here tonight is in a good humour. And why not? This game promises to be . . .*"

Apple went on listening with reduced attention while he steered at high speed between the twin lines of cars. Traffic, which had been dense, grew sparser as suburbia gradually became countryside.

But there were still enough walking or riding observers of his noisy passing to make Apple feel obliged to assist it. He wore a grim, ambulanceman expression.

". . . has just been located. It was somewhere else, not in the auditorium here. A small fault, it seems, which will be put right before you can say Jack O'Robinson."

Apple daren't go faster. Already the ambulance was weaving and shuddering, as well as nearly going into skids on the wet tarmac whenever a bend was taken.

Beneath his tension, however, Apple was enjoying himself. His lifelong speeding-with-siren wish had always been as strong as the next man's, and he found that realisation was no disappointment, despite the fact that his vehicle wasn't a fire engine.

". . . sabotage has been whispered. But it's practically inevitable that someone would try to get melodrama into the situation. I'm sure that there's nothing wrong here at Harp Hall except some minor . . ."

The ambulance left the last suburban villa behind. There were no more lighted windows or porches to break up the darkness which lay back from the headlights. Traffic was reduced to the occasional car.

Apple felt the lack of observers. Some of the shine went out of the ride.

Without warning, a sign appeared. It named and pointed the way to West Town's private flying club. Apple braked and swung the steering-wheel.

Unsurprisingly, the ambulance went into a skid, a long one, which took it on past the turning. The vehicle also turned completely around. But the road was deserted at that moment, and Apple was able to keep from crashing into anything on either side.

Even before the ambulance stopped, he was urging it in the

other direction, his head and shoulders making short swoops forward. The rear wheels spun on the wetness, then gripped. Tyres squealed briefly as they were brutalised ahead.

"*. . . crowd getting somewhat impatient here at Harp Hall, ladies and gentlemen. And for those of you who have tuned in late, let me explain that the game hasn't started yet. Lighting over the court . . .*"

At a reasonable speed, Apple made the turning. He came onto a driveway. It was lined with pine trees and fed to a broad, low building.

The roots of the trees having created a wavy road surface, the ambulance began to buck like a camel.

Even so, Apple was unable to bring himself to slow still further. He went on being tossed around until the driveway smoothed, which happened as it widened out into a circle in front of the club building.

Its windows were all dark. Not that Apple was interested in this part of the club. He drove on, speeding up, and went around the building's side.

His headlights led the way between two rusty Nissen huts, then shot off into empty blackness. It was too late, Apple thought with a hollow sense of loss.

He swung the wheel—and gave a canine grin. Directly ahead, several hundred yards away, stood a small aircraft, with beside it a mini-bus, and with between the two a group of men.

That the group was small—five strong—Apple had expected. Dui had said the deal would be played down by the KGB, who, additionally, would want no hint of pressure should this all fall apart.

Apple put his foot down. The radio commentator interrupted himself to say, "*Ah, the problem has been solved.*"

Apple raced across the cinder airfield. His siren was still clamouring, his yellow light still whirled. The men had turned to stare. As well as the basketball stars, there was a man in ordinary clothes and one in a flying suit. All were protected from the rain by a broad, high wing.

Apple brought the ambulance to a sliding halt across the front of the aircraft. When he switched the ignition off, motor and siren died; everything else stayed on.

Apple alighted quickly. As he strode the dozen paces to where the stretched-out group stood, he noted everyone's position.

The pilot was by a short flight of concertina steps that tongued out of the plane's doorway. The main confrontation appeared to be between the plain-clothes Hammer and the stars; they stood three facing one, players with their backs to the mini-bus, Hammer between there and the steps.

Recognising Apple, the British athletes all began talking at him. In general, they wanted to know what the hell was going on here. They sounded neither worried nor angry, merely a shade bemused.

Apple paid them scant attention. He was fully occupied with the Hammer, who had a flat face and greased-down hair and who was easing forward. Improbably, he held one hand inside his coat. He looked frustrated and furious, as well as cheap.

Going toward him, Apple started speaking. The language he used was Russian. That brought the athletes to a sudden silence. It brought the Hammer to a stooping, wary stop, and the pilot to a rough-and-ready sort of attention.

What Apple said was, "All right, comrade, I'll take over from here. These men're needed elsewhere. Your efforts will be discussed some other time and in another place. Take that bus back where you found it."

The bluff didn't work. His features tense, the Hammer said, "I have a gun inside my coat."

"Rubbish," Apple scoffed. "Anyone knows that gag."

The Hammer produced a gun. He said, "Thanks for attending. You're just what we wanted. Now explain to these idiots that this is their aircraft, whether the lady's here or not. Tell them to get in."

Still moving slowly, Apple tried again with "Comrade Karpov is in trouble."

"As you will be yourself if you don't do what I say and immediately."

"Which was what? I've forgotten."

The Hammer grated, "Tell them to get in the plane."

Apple hesitated. He felt there was no real threat to himself from the gun, or any danger of the team stars actually getting aboard the aircraft—unless it be at gunpoint. Shortage of time was the only problem.

Even so, Apple stretched out his hesitation. He liked the scene. He was delighted to be a part of it: these machines and men being flicked at regular intervals with yellow light, and with a radio mumbling in the background and with himself edging closer to the armed KGB agent.

One of the athletes spoke. Then the others joined in. They barraged:

"What is all this, Teever?"

"I hope that's not a real gun."

"Where's the emergency?"

"What's that bloody lingo you're jabbering?"

"Just what're you playing at, Teever, and who is this odd character?"

While they were barraging, the Hammer shouted a shut-up

in Russian and the pilot scowled as if because of not knowing what else he could do.

"Everything's going to be fine," Apple said. He was now within contactable distance of the Hammer, of whom he asked in the other's language, "Isn't that right, you stinking goat?"

"Huh?"

The verbal diversion sufficed as a cue for Apple. He threw himself over the remaining space. Passingly, he wondered which he felt as the most important, to disarm the Hammer or to look good in this onstage situation.

The routine was simple. Apple had done it a hundred times before, but only against gym-opponents whose weapons had been dummies.

Now he was acutely aware of the difference as he swung himself around right in front of the Hammer, so that his back was to him, while simultaneously grabbing for the wrist of the gun-holding hand.

The Russian agent was fast. At the same time as he drew his right arm back, away from the grab, he threw his left forward in a punch to the kidneys.

The resulting slam of pain caused Apple to twist about, which, conveniently, brought him again within reach of the gun. He flung at it with both hands; one missed, the other raked its fingernails over flesh.

Blood spurted. The man gasped. His fingers opened. The revolver dropped.

The Soviet agent's superior speed worked against him this time. He was the first to stoop toward his gun, beginning almost before it had landed on the cinders. His reflexes were perfect.

Therefore Apple couldn't help feeling that it was somehow unfair, the way he had nothing more to do than crash down a rabbit-punch on the nape of his opponent's neck.

The KGB man dropped like an armful of dough. He lay still. The whole battle had taken some eight or ten seconds.

Apple straightened and turned. In the faces of the stars, he read respect peeking through the dislike and surprise. He shuffled his shoulders toughly.

"All right, men," he said in a crisp tone, "get yourselves in that ambulance. Quick." He pointed sternly, like a parent at a doorway.

Lazily, the player called Wayne asked, "What for?"

Apple's arm sagged. "So I can rush you back to Harp Hall, of course. There's time if we hurry. Maybe the game hasn't started yet."

"Of course it hasn't. There's an emergency on."

"It's finished," Apple said, exasperated. "It's all over. But wait. I'll turn the radio higher, then you can—"

The three stars, Apple realised, had shifted their attention. Flicking his head around, he saw that the pilot (whose presence had slipped his mind) was about to roll the Hammer over. The revolver lay underneath.

Apple moved in attackingly. As he did, the pilot shot up straight. They tangled above the prone body, over which Apple then tripped as he was pulled in that direction. He sprawled onto the man in the flying suit, who promptly collapsed under the weight.

As they fell together, Apple bumped his nose on the man's brow; and, as they were rolling over like fighting schoolboys, he saw through waterlogged vision that the British athletes were watching with interest.

Apple shouted at them, "Take the ambulance. Go straight to the stadium."

"No, thanks," Wayne said. "Not if that's where this emergency is."

"The radio," Apple called, punching and grappling. "Turn it up. You'll see. No emergency."

Nobody moved. Wayne asked with less laziness, "Then, what's all this about?"

Another man: "And why all the violence?"

The third athlete took a turn with "And why did that bloke bring us here?"

"Exactly, Teever," Wayne said. "And just who the bloody hell are you, anyway?"

"This is no time for questions," Apple gasped. He was quietly furious at not being able to do better in this ridiculous wrestling match, for the pilot was obviously not KGB: his unarmed-combat knowledge was severely limited.

From the Hammer came a groan. It wasn't the first, though by far the loudest. The man's recovery seemed imminent.

Apple said quickly, "Listen. I'll tell you. But I shouldn't. I'll be blowing my cover."

"Cover?" Wayne said. "Go on."

"I'm from Scotland Yard. The anti-terrorist squad. I was sent with you people because of a threat from the Irish Republican Army. I'm a cop. I know nothing of basketball. I've never played it in my life."

"Balls," one of the men said.

Shuffling, the Hammer mumbled.

Apple: "Somebody move that man and get his gun."

Wayne: "You do it."

"I'm busy."

"For all we know, he's on our side."

"He's IRA, you fool," Apple spat. He had bits of cinder in his mouth. "So is this one. Did they speak English to you? Of course not. They can't. They only know Gaelic. What did you think we were talking—bloody Russian?"

When there was no answer to that, Apple pressed on with "Did any of you ever see me play basketball? Or practicing? Or even holding a ball in my hands?"

None of the athletes spoke. The Hammer whimpered and moved his head.

"I came to Ireland to help protect you people," Apple panted. He and the pilot lay side by side, exchanging aborted clutches and fumbled punches.

One of the players asked, "Is the game really due to start?"

"Turn the radio up. You'll see. There was a delay because of an electrical fault. But all that can be explained later. *Move,* someone. Do you want your reserves to lose this game?"

That brought a little action. One of the men broke rank, ran to the ambulance and reached inside to the dashboard.

". . . not only first-blood that went to this fine group of lads from East Germany," the commentator was saying. *"It's all unexpected. But the game's in its infancy yet. Anything can happen, as we . . ."*

Hollowly, Wayne said, "They're playing."

Apple would have given some version of an I-told-you-so except that the pilot had a hold on his neck. He gurgled.

". . . which brings the score to six. That's six to nothing in favour of the East Germans."

Apple broke the hold. "There's still time," he said. "They're only six points ahead."

"Only?" Wayne said. "You really *don't* know anything about basketball, do you?"

"I told you so."

"Christ," one of the athletes said. "Six to bubbles. We're being demolished."

". . . yes indeed," the commentator said. *"And here comes an-*

other, I think. Yes. A truly fine shot, bringing the score up to seven–zero."

As one man, the basketball stars jumped to action. But coordination ended there. Wayne started to board the mini-bus, one man went toward the ambulance, the remaining player set off running across the cinders but turned back almost at once.

"Help!" Apple shouted, struggling with the rank amateur. "Get this savage off me!"

One skirmishing minute later, all organised, Apple and the stars were shooting away in the ambulance. Pilot and Hammer had been bundled aboard the aircraft, revolver had been hurled into the darkness, ignition key had been removed from the mini-bus and tossed onto its roof.

Most time during that one minute had been spent, at its latter part, with the four tall men squabbling over who should drive. After firmly, even belligerently, pointing out that he was by far the oldest, in addition to being the one who had brought the ambulance in the first place, Apple had won.

He sat now squarely at the steering-wheel, with one man beside him and the other two leaning over from behind. Attention was split: passengers' on the radio commentator, driver's on the way ahead.

Apple reached the pair of Nissen huts. As he sped between them, he decided on his plan in respect of arrival at Harp Hall.

To avoid explanations to various members of the United Kingdom sports contingent, to the police, to fellow spooks and to one irate para-medic, he would stop the ambulance a couple of hundred yards short of the rear entrance, then make a run for it into the suburban darkness and desertion. Within minutes he would be with Dui at the car.

Roaring around onto the tree-lined driveway, Apple bounced

himself and the others about while battering on over the surface lumpiness. That survived, he curved out onto the highway, where he slammed his foot to the floor.

Only one vehicle was approaching within clear view. Apple was not the least bit surprised to see that it was a police patrol car; nor to hear, as he roared by it, that its brakes were squealing.

Next, through his rear-view mirror, he saw the patrol car make a fast U-turn. Its flash-light and siren came on, matching those of the ambulance.

Apple settled to driving.

This, he mused, almost in disbelief, could not be topped. It was wild but true. Here he sat, Appleton Porter, the core of a real drama. He was the commando rescue-squad, the cavalry and the returning hero all rolled into one. He was, you might say, a Churchill, saviour of his nation in its hour of need.

Apple ignored the fact that if it hadn't been for his interventions, the hour of need would never have arrived. He had stopped thinking. He didn't even think of the sensuous prize that would follow.

Apple was living this moment, this final scene, to its fullest and richest.

He saw the lights flashing, the cars scuttling out of his way, the people gaping; he heard the sirens, the commentator's tense voice, the listening stars' muffled groans and gasps; he felt the thrill of the chase, the excitement of high speed, the ambience of urgency.

Glittering along at eighty miles an hour, Apple supposed that he had a stiff upper lip and a steely gaze. In reality, his Irish lip was slack and his English eyes were smiling.

CHAPTER 7

"Are you comfortable?"

"Mmmmmore or less."

"If there's something wrong . . ."

"Well, would you mind if I bent my legs?"

"Why, I'd be delighted—because then I could bend mine."

As they both drew their feet inside the tent and out of the rain, they said in fair unison, "It's so good to be with someone who understands."

About the Author

Marc Lovell is the author of seven previous Appleton Porter novels, including *The Only Good Apple in a Barrel of Spies, How Green Was My Apple* and *Apple Spy in the Sky,* which will soon be released as the film *Trouble at the Royal Rose.* He has lived on the island of Majorca for over twenty years.